THE
SLIP

THE SLIP

stories

MIRIAM WEBSTER

Aniko

Published by Aniko Press 2025

Book design and typesetting:
Duncan Blachford, Typography Studio
Author photo: Bonnie Jarrett Creative

Aniko Press acknowledges Australia's First Nations peoples as the traditional owners and custodians of this country, and we pay our respects to their elders, past and present.

978-0-6489898-0-6 (paperback)
978-0-6489898-1-3 (ebook)

Catalogue records for this book are available from the National Library of Australia.

anikopress.com

CONTENTS

CONTENTS

Life's nonsense pierces us with strange relation.

WALLACE STEVENS

Only the scorned and the ridiculous make good stories.

DJUNA BARNES

GLIMMER

THIS MORNING THERE IS dirty seafoam like a coffee stain along the lip of the shore. It trembles and collapses, calling to mind the time you had an affair with a married man. You walk along the beach, sometimes kicking up the abject froth so that it flies off in the wind, remembering how it happened. It was a while ago now, but you still think of him from time to time.

Next year, you will graduate. The creative writing program has taught you that the best short stories should contain a single grain of truth. You have learned to use bright adjectives and dynamic phrasing. You are supposed to be poised and precise. You are supposed to write what you know. Well, what do you know? You know that love has always been the most compelling source of knowledge in your life. You want to write about the affair but worry that your story, your imperative, is deeply unoriginal.

One of your creative writing teachers says originality is a redundant category: all contemporary writing, she says, *already suffers from the affliction of intertextual polyvocality.* You consider this and kick up seafoam. If you wrote it, you would have to change some names and dates and places. If you wrote it, it might begin like this.

ONE FRIDAY THERE'S A party after work to celebrate the acquisition of a new, important manuscript. You work for a publishing company although you're not a publisher, just one of the girls from Reception. Mostly, people look down on you. The women are too busy doing all the work to pay you much attention and the men are like most others. An older gentleman has asked you why you dress like a dolly. A junior publisher dropped a highlighter in between your breasts, claiming it was accidental. Another one, the man who hired you, said that it's good to keep the pretty girls at Reception because it makes the business seem successful.

The man in question is different. If he thinks these things, he doesn't say them. He is exceptionally tall, with very dark hair and very light eyes, a combination of extremes. His features don't quite fit together, which makes him handsome in a peculiar way. And there is something unsettled in his carriage too; he seems skittish, a strange mix of confidence and nerves. You don't know when it was that you first noticed him, but as he steps out of the lift tonight, he smiles.

The party is something you've helped organise and you are anxious for the whole thing to go well. You take photos of the happy revellers for the company's socials, greet important guests and in the downtime drink champagne to calm your nerves. You should probably slow down but it's expensive stuff, the kind you can't afford, and you want to drink as much of it as possible. At some point in the night you catch his eye across the room and after that you can't stop looking at each other. Furtively at first, and then with open wanting.

There are speeches to be made about the book. It's the next big thing, a book of essays written by a hot young writer with a slick resume. Most of the essays are about partying, fucking, art and the sublime. The writer arrives dressed in black, sulks beautifully and never smiles, even though this must be one of the most important nights of his life. Everyone wants a photo. Marketing is palpably excited about adding his book to the company's vibrant queer collection.

Even though you're just a receptionist, you are not without your wiles. You persuaded one of the publishing assistants to let you read an advance copy and believe the book will be successful, even if its transgressions are more aesthetic than exciting. Still, you liked the bit about the birth of Aphrodite, how Kronos castrates his father Uranus and throws his balls into the sea, which roils mightily and churns itself to froth, and out from the foam pops Aphrodite. *Aphros* is actually the Greek word for seafoam, which turns out not to be a benign substance but the residue, so the writer argues, of erotic excess.

Eros is catching.

Professional standards are cast aside like useless garments and the night becomes debauched. A blonde woman takes her shoes off and starts dancing on the table. The bosses bring out more champagne. Singles start to couple and uncouple, while established couples take on thirds and fourths. In this spirit, you and the man flirt shamelessly. He invites you for a cigarette and you follow him down to the car park, where he licks the TALLY-HO paper and desire bubbles up like something primordial in your loins. Yes, you'll use the word loins, because it's funny and accurate. You will ask him if he's read the book, but do not be deterred when he says he found it *unoriginal*.

'Any wanker with an arts degree could have written that.'

'Do you have an arts degree?'

'English Lit. I thought I wanted to write novels—' he drags on his cigarette, then offers it to you, 'but they quickly beat that out of me.'

You're not sure what he means about the beating, although you're titillated by its kinky undertone. The way he laughs about his failed dream is quite endearing. 'You must have read a lot,' you say, all drunk and googly-eyed. 'You must be a really great reader.'

He shrugs, finishes his cigarette. Then he steps right up and kisses you. To think that any minute someone might come down to get their car and spring you! He pulls you in and kisses you harder. It is difficult to breathe. You make out for a while and then he says he should go home.

Afterward, remember how he said *I want you*. You want him to say it again, even if it's cheesy. Start noticing things that rhyme with *I want you*, many of them to do with cheese: *cheese fondue, danablu, brocciu*. But also, *seafood stew, beef ragu, pad see ew*. Oh yes, you want him to eat you all up! Would he be a noisy chewer or a silent one? Fear noisy. Dream the two of you are on a beach when a storm whips up a great big wash of seafoam and the man says he is hungry and bends down, suddenly, to scoop a palmful of foam into his mouth. *I want you and your seafoam, too*. What a weird dream. You wake and masturbate energetically, foaming and gushing like a mythical sea.

Monday morning: everyone at the office looks seedy or sheepish. You send an email on the office server, something admin related though covertly suggestive, and when he replies you agree to meet for drinks.

You arrive at the appointed spot a little early, which makes you seem overeager, and then he is late, which makes you think he isn't coming. Clinging to the bar stool as the corporate crowd gets drunk and then goes home for dinner, you read your book and try looking serene, as if reading alone in bars is just something you do. Think: I am cool. I am a very cool person.

About forty minutes later, just as the date is beginning to seem lost, he walks in wearing cowboy boots. 'I'm sorry,' he says, 'we couldn't get the kids to sleep.'

It's distinctly unsexy, as far as openers go, but you can't help admiring his bold choice of footwear. His jeans are lightly tucked to expose the high stiff leg, the tall curvaceous heel and shining cherry leather; they make him stand a little taller. He looks sexy and desperate: a hot literary cowboy part way through a midlife crisis.

'You look familiar,' he says.

'Do I know you?' You look around the room. 'Have we met before?'

He gives you an indulgent smile. 'What are you reading?'

It is Lorrie Moore's *Self Help*; the first story is called 'How to Be an Other Woman.' Allow yourself a nervous smile. Tell him that the narrator is sharing a Reuben sandwich with her colleague, making a lot of tragic puns.

'Yeah, I've read it,' he says. 'Not really my thing.'

Feel embarrassed. Accept his offer to bring you, next time, *something better to read*.

A routine is established: he lends you books and you interpret his reasons for lending them as you would decipher code. He prefers the type of künstlerroman which has gained cachet in recent years; it's your suspicion that he fancies himself a secret Knausgaard or perhaps a Cusk. Even more than this, the man admires feminist autotheory, and you can't decide whether this is evidence of his good taste or a studied pose to get you into bed.

In any case, it is an education. While reading, you take a pencil and underline suggestive passages. You spend a lot of time with *I Love Dick*, trying to impress and arouse him with your coy marginalia. At other times your messaging is pretty obvious, such as when you underline, in *Chelsea Girls*, I only like getting drunk and being in love. Above all, you understand what Maggie Nelson means when she writes about the pulsing of a pussy in great need of fucking. You know that he will flip through the book when you return it and read your desire all the way through.

For the sake of character development, consider the difference in age. He is older than you by fourteen years; enough to make it thrilling for being hardly inappropriate.

Sometimes you think of his domestic life, the one he carries on without you. It is easy enough to look up his address at work; coincidentally, it is not far from your house. Walking to the shops one day, you cannot help but travel past it. There is a lemon tree, an SUV, a family of bicycles, some planter boxes and a cubby house in the front yard. A fluffy cat sits in the window, glaring. You hate his car. You hate his cat. You wish you hadn't gone there. From now on, even when your curiosity is meowing at the window, do not ask about his artist wife and two small children, whose names are Sebastian and Claudette. Glean this in passing, like any good mistress. But don't think of yourself as his mistress, because that character arc is limiting and has been way overdone.

Instead, think about your part in a long hysterical you mean historical tradition. As an aspiring writer it's a rite of passage. You're in it for the story. You're gonna write the next Karenina or Bovary or whatever, this is an experiment, it's autotheory; you're Chris fucking Kraus.

Sex itself is hard to coordinate; in fact, you've not got around to *doing it* at all. That's fine – deferred pleasure creates narrative tension, multiplying and sustaining it, urging it toward an exquisite, unbearable climax. Whenever it gets too much, relieve this tension with steamy kissing scenes in one of the usual locations: cars, bars, shady alcoves on frigid nights when your mouths are hot and hungry and the air glitters with July mists.

Walking home from these encounters, warm despite the chill. Taking off your jacket thinking how it all makes sense, the books and poetry, the lies and exaltations, even though you can't explain it to your sisters or your friends. Sneaking around, guarding your perfect little secret, confirmed in your opinion that life is not about what you achieve but what you can get away with.

Weeks pass.

You steal glances at work, smoke in the car park and occasionally touch. One day you ride the lift together and he kisses you, swiftly and intensely, before the doors open on your floor. You meet in bars and drink. You send some sexy emails where you each describe, in heightened formal language, all the ways you'd like to suck and fuck each other basically to death. You think you'll die of wanting. Nothing's really happening, and yet you've never lived as greedily as now.

It's time to coax the narrative to crisis. This part might involve some liberties with the truth but that's okay since this is fiction. You have grown a little sick of waiting when he finally emails with the news that his wife and kids are visiting her mother in another city. *Meet me after work tomorrow*, he writes, *and I'll dash you off to my country estate.*

The next day he picks you up and drives you down the coast in a hired car. Why the hired car? You assume he wants no trace of you discoverable in his own car, like a stray hair or bobby pin, or the wrapper from an ice cream he wouldn't normally choose. (Wives always know which ice cream their husbands choose.)

Scenery passes by the window. You try to make small talk but he is taciturn and preoccupied. This makes you anxious. You try to think of conversation points but can't decide which ones are right.

'How long have you been married?'

He pauses. 'We've been together since we were sixteen. Yeah, I know. It's lame.'

'No, I think it's … I think it's …' but you can't think of what to say. 'So have you ever, like, done this before?'

'What? Snuck off down the beach with a beautiful young woman? Not exactly. I've had—'

'Affairs?'

'Kind of. Not really. Affairs of the lips, maybe. Affairs of the heart. But I've never, well …' he trails off.

Both of you are silent for the rest of the drive. Pretend it didn't give you the ick when he said 'affairs of the lips.' Pretend that everything is fine. Ignore it when his wife rings and he takes the call over the Bluetooth speaker, urgently miming for you to be silent so as not to give yourself away. Ignore the humiliation. Ignore your better judgement, which is used to your neglect.

By the time you arrive it is dark. The driveway to the house is overgrown and everything feels haunted.

'Do you come here often?' you ask doubtfully. 'How long have you had this place?'

'It's Trisha's. Her dad left it to us when he died.'

Inside, there are pictures of her as a child next to pictures of their children. There are hats and raincoats hanging in the hall. There are boogie boards in the garage. Her shoes are lined up next to the front door. Her feet are smaller than yours and all her shoes are dainty; little boots and pretty sandals. You want to ask him why she dresses like a doll. Instead you say, 'Nice digs. But ah, I think we have a problem. It's a little warm in here.'

'Oh really?'

'Yeah. I think I'm wearing too much clothing.'

He looks concerned. 'Are you uncomfortable? Here, I'll turn the heating down.'

'Wait, no, I'm fine. Take off my coat.'

He unbuttons it. Underneath, you're wearing only lingerie. 'Wow,' he says, standing back and looking at you. 'This is … this is …'

'What?'

'I'm sorry. I'm just really tired. Can we leave it 'til the morning?'

He gives you a chaste kiss on the forehead and shows you upstairs. In the bathroom, you brush your teeth side by side like a couple in the movies, you still in your coat and lingerie and him in his pyjamas. Struggle with a sense of unreality. Try not to laugh. Try not to cry. They are navy blue with pizzas on them. Try not to see this as depressing and absurd.

You go to sleep spooning, which is nice, but you keep wondering if you're sleeping on her side. He says he's happy that you're here. 'Thanks for coming,' he whispers, 'I'm so happy that you're here.'

'Me too,' you say. 'I'm really glad I came.'

But then you wake in the night feeling disoriented and lonely. You feel the biggest, widest, most impossible loneliness you've ever felt. Beside you he is sleeping deeply and you feel that in this sleep he has abandoned you.

In the morning you feel irritable and ill-used.

You decide to nurture this feeling – he is married, after all. So you stoke resentment's mean little fires, even when he gives you the best head you've ever received. You nurture it even when you have sex in the shower and afterward he washes your hair using fancy shampoo, which foams madly and smells like flowers, and his body feels so nice against yours in the warm slip of the water, and he *wants you wants you wants you*, and his eyes are burning blue.

At breakfast he chews loudly, eating muesli like a horse shoving its head into a bag of oats. Between mouthfuls, he tries to initiate a boring conversation about some colleagues. While he munches, watch his mouth and try to muster up some feeling, either affectionate or sexual, but end with indifference. The day outside looks freezing, and as you gaze out at the bitter morning, desire leaks from you and puddles at your feet.

Feeling desperate, you try to shake things up by doing a kind of burlesque with the croissants, rubbing a butter knife over your nipples and being naughty with the jam. You giggle and flounce, lolling across his lap like the nude Parisian girls you saw once with your friend at Crazy Horse. He asks you what you're doing and you say, 'Would you like to butter my croissant?'

Now he's talking about his children. He can't help it – he misses them, it's the first time he's been away from the baby for more than a day. It's pathetic. 'Call me baby,' you suddenly say.

'What?'

'I want you to call me baby. I'll call you Daddy.'

Despite himself his face is flirting with a smile. 'Don't. It's not funny.'

Say, 'But it's not *not* funny, is it Daddy?'

'What's wrong with you?' he asks. 'Why are you being weird?'

Keep calling him Daddy until his smile is completely gone. He ignores you and starts texting. You realise that the two of you have nothing in common besides books, longing and a vague sense of shared dissatisfaction.

The morning continues darkly and from time to time it rains. Trisha calls again and while he's talking on the phone you slip into her raincoat, which smells faintly of BO; it's almost like wearing her skin. Feeling like another woman, walk toward the beach, the mist like spittle on your face. What the fuck have you been thinking? On the one hand, your romantic getaway is turning out to be a load of shit. On the other, you can admit you are a bit in love with him already. It's impossible. You don't know what to do.

On the cliffs the wind is powerful. You breathe in and out, feeling it pummel the muscles of your face. Down below the waves are aggro and piratical, pillaging the sand. You descend the steps and then you see it: seafoam, huge swathes of it, so thick and pale and vast that the entire beach seems covered in new-fallen snow.

Exhilarated, struck with nauseous wonder, you walk back to the house thinking you will give the thing another go.

In the loungeroom he is sitting in a sulky pose and reading, so you cuddle up beside him on the couch, open the Lorrie Moore again and try to make things feel congenial. The narrator is sad because it's been a week since her lover has called. The next time he phones he says, 'I was having a dream about you and suddenly I woke up with a jerk and felt very uneasy.' The narrator says, 'Yeah, I hate waking up with jerks.'

You look over at the man. He can be such a jerk. If you were his wife, you would probably find this endearing. Perhaps it *is* endearing. You draw his arm around you, kissing his fingers one by one.

'What's funny?' he asks.

'Just the book.'

'You're still reading that?' He sighs and shifts over, so that your bodies aren't touching anymore.

'What's wrong with it? What's your problem?'

He chooses his next words carefully. 'Maybe it appeals to someone with your experience of life. But you learn things as you get older, you don't find the same things funny as before. You joke a lot, and I wonder if it's because you're insecure.'

'I don't know why I joke.' You suddenly feel very small.

'I'm sorry. It will get easier.' Then he kisses your head in a way that is distinctly fatherly.

You look up at him with big, childish eyes. 'Thanks ... Daddy.' And without meaning to you suddenly let loose one long, loud snort of laughter.

He looks at you.

'What the fuck is wrong with you,' he says, and reaches for his phone.

You read once that <u>humour has a history of belonging to men</u>. The problem is that he thinks you're insecure and you're beginning to admit that he's a wanker. Now he is texting his wife again. 'They're coming home early,' he says. 'Shit. Get your stuff, we really need to go.'

Leaving makes you wild with a kind of grief you've never felt before. He drives again while you stare out the window, the same scenery as yesterday passing by, only now there is a rainbow. Imagine prolonging the relationship, you try to reason, waiting months or even years for him to say he's finally left his wife.

Is that what you want?

He will say, 'I've left my wife for you,' placing emphasis on the *you*, and once this happens you'll be responsible for his happiness and the fallout with his family, his friends and all his networks. Both of you will have to find another job and when he doesn't find one, you will have to be supportive. Trisha will kick him out and he will move into your share house, where you'll find him sitting on the futon in his crumpled shirt and cowboy boots, talking to your stoner housemate Frida about art, watching Scandinavian crime dramas and eating a whole box of ice creams, the ones he likes, the ones that Trisha knows to buy him, dropping the wrappers on the floor. Come on! You're young. You're fun. You're full of ...

You've got so much life ahead of you!

Back in Brunswick, he drops you out the front of your share house, where your housemates are on the porch drinking, smoking and carrying on because it's Saturday afternoon. You look over at them wistfully, torn between two worlds.

'Sorry about all this,' he says, looking genuinely remorseful. 'Things haven't been great between me and Trisha lately. I mean, it's been a long time coming. Meeting you has obviously changed things and I'm starting to think ...' A misty look comes over him. He clasps your head between his hands. You can tell he is about to say it, and the thought fills you with dread.

'Please don't,' you mumble, snatching all your stuff and getting out. You steal a glance at your housemates, who have paused their revelry to watch. Then you lean in through the window, and yes, you're doing it, you're ending the affair.

For the next few days you weep, mope and keep one of his books as a memento. Moving on is both easier and more painful than you thought.

PRESENT DAY, PRESENT MOMENT: you're sitting at your computer. You left the publishing company and do not miss it. You are living with another man and you have your writing degree. When the book deal comes through, you feel a pressing urge to tell the man with whom you had an affair. He sends you a bottle of prosecco in the mail which is misdirected before it finds you. Inside the box is a handwritten note. His handwriting – you never saw it before. You stare at it and somehow, it moves you.

For a moment you consider *what could have been*, concluding that the passion which once heaved inside you like a wave has now retreated, moon-drawn, from a shore that cannot hold it. Perhaps he'd like the look of this wave, retreating from this shore, if it appeared in one of those books he loves. It's funny, isn't it, how these things go? Because this will always be the first thing you ever wrote, and you would like to thank him, after all that passed between you, for his small part in your becoming.

Here is that wave.

You watch it draw back gently, gently, until all that remains on the beach is a faint glimmer of seafoam.

MOVEMENTS
OF THE SOUL

ON FRIDAY EVENING JOY goes to the housewarming party of a woman she met at the dog park. She is asked to bring a plate and goes to a lot of trouble making this elaborate salad she pulled from an Ottolenghi book. When she arrives, the table is laden with other people's offerings, but as Joy places hers between them she feels stupid for going to such lengths; everyone else has just brought plates of kabana, tasty cheese and supermarket dip.

The host is a woman with wild hennaed hair and a psycho kelpie-cross gone mad from lack of work. She gives Joy a hug and introduces her to a pair of women talking. Pleasantries are exchanged, but after a while the women resume their conversation from before. Joy drifts away from them as if it's accidental. Meanwhile, the kelpie-cross runs laps around them, yelping and occasionally nipping people's heels.

The downstairs toilet is smaller than a cupboard. Joy slips in there to hide and notices a sign above the cistern which reads *Please flush sparingly, we're running on tank water* ☺ . She scowls. Some animal has taken this instruction literally and left a huge shit in the bowl. Joy grabs the toilet gel, douses and begins to scrub, cursing the woman from the dog park, her filthy guests and crap food and her pass-agg smiley face. She doesn't even really like her, this person who constantly talks about her menopause and doesn't seem to understand her dog at all. Why did she come here? Maybe it's a crisis, she thinks and flushes. Maybe she is finally having a midlife crisis.

Shortly after her fifty-fifth birthday, Joy was made redundant. She'd been promised a promotion, but when the architecture firm restructured, a man was given it instead. Her friend Judy took her out for lunch to commiserate; they ate Middle Eastern food and talked about their daughters. Bowls and plates of gleaming mezze filled the table, more food than they could eat, and Joy rushed through the meal with singular speed until she felt suddenly, immensely full. Judy's plate remained untouched as she shared pictures of her eldest, who had just been selected to play in the oldest symphonic orchestra in the American Ivy League. Judy is a barrister and her daughter is at Harvard. This really shouldn't matter, but it does.

Her only consolation is that Judy's daughter looks like a sloth and plays the piccolo flute, which is absurd. The photos are embarrassing. Joy's own daughter is wonderful and has just released her second studio album, even though she's only twenty-one. The two girls played in school band together – that's how she knows Judy.

At the end of the meal Judy became absorbed in her phone again, replying to emails, giving Joy the distinct impression she planned on ignoring the bill entirely until Joy took out her credit card and paid, even though it was supposed to be Judy's treat. She felt extremely hostile towards her as they stood outside the restaurant saying goodbye, Judy waiting for an Uber, traffic blaring, pigeons milling at their feet. As she was getting in the Camry, Judy looked at Joy meaningfully and asked how she was going.

'No I mean – *really*. Have you found another job? What have you been doing since they *dumped* you?'

Such a harsh way of saying it, thought Joy, like throwing something bulky from the window of a car.

'Not yet,' said Joy. 'I'm considering my options.'

'God it must be so *awful*. How are you *surviving*? Do you have *anything* to occupy your time?'

Fuck Judy, the stingy bitch. On the tram home, Joy decided she needed better friends.

So now she's at this party, but there is no one here she wants to talk to. Once the toilet's clean, she shuts the door and has a snoop around the house. There's some bad art in the master bedroom which the hostess must have made herself, a couple of wacko sculptures involving piles of toothpicks, painted seeds and stacks of dried orange peel. She hates it, but the room smells beautifully of citrus.

Outside, the summer light is falling. Joy goes back upstairs. On the staircase, which is extremely narrow, she passes by a younger man. He wears a dark expression which disappears when he sees her, as if she has startled the trouble from his face. They do an awkward dance but can't help pressing together, so close she feels the buckle of his belt against her stomach, silvery and cold. A quick thrill passes through her. The man is very tall and dresses like he's famous. He looks to be in his late twenties, medium build, with lank brown hair styled limply in a mullet. His complexion suggests a lack of health, although she quickly likes his eyes, which are dark and bright like a person with fever.

Later in the night, having downed an entire bottle of rosé, Joy feels like flirting. She goes up to the younger man she squeezed past on the staircase, who is talking to a group around the fire, to ask how he knows the hostess. He says he teaches music with her at the polytechnic. 'So you're a musician,' Joy says coquettishly, dragging a hand along his arm. To her gratification, the man does not retreat. 'I am,' he says. 'You look familiar. Are you a muso too?'

'Oh no,' says Joy. 'I'm practically tone deaf. My daughter is, but she got that from her dad. You could say I have a type.'

'How old's your daughter,' he asks.

Joy falters for a moment. 'She's only twenty-one.'

'Oh, just a baby. God, I remember when I was twenty-one. I did not have my shit together at all.' He gives her a penetrating look. 'So you have a type, hey? Does it apply to all musicians, or do they have to play a certain instrument?'

'Mostly guitarists, I guess.'

'Must be my lucky night,' he says.

'Oh really?' Joy smiles. 'But can you make love to a woman as well as you make love to your guitar?'

'I guess it depends on what type of body she has. You know ... rosewood, maple, mahogany.'

They laugh, their tone light, but there's a serious game being played.

They go on like this until the fire's low and some of the other guests are leaving. The hostess tries to crash their conversation, putting her hands all over the younger man, trying to coax him into the bedroom to admire one of her awful sculptures, and some of the other women at the party glance at them furtively, trying to ascertain what's going on. Joy takes a secret pleasure in knowing that the man's in high demand. He brushes the hostess off politely and, with a conspiratorial smile, comes back to stand with Joy.

'I never asked – how do you know Maggie?'

'Oh,' she says vaguely. 'I don't, really. I just met her at the dog park.'

'Want to get out of here?' he asks.

Joy says yes and it is done.

HIS HOUSE IS IN a gentrified suburb by the Merri Creek where lots of social workers, lesbians and music teachers live. Joy stands behind while he unlocks the door, looking at his high round buttocks, feeling momentarily self-conscious. She should go back to Pilates. That's it – after this weekend she's buying a membership to the gym.

They walk down a narrow hallway and Joy realises that she doesn't know his name. Too late. The other bedroom doors are closed and she imagines who else lives here. The thought passes. Now they are in his bedroom and he's taking off his shirt, revealing a body that is young and firm, a little underweight, but in a sinewy way she associates with rock'n'roll. She removes hers too and things happen quickly after that; they have a natural chemistry. The only thing that bothers her is that he wants to make intense, lingering eye contact. It's not off-putting per se, but it makes her think that he is trying too hard to connect.

Afterward he wraps his arm around her waist possessively, snuggling her into the hollow of his body. The endorphins wear off and a dull headache thuds behind her eyes, her gut revolts, she is prematurely hungover. As he falls asleep the young man's arm gets heavy and begins to crush her ribs. Unwillingly, she thinks of the breakdown of her partnership, the sleepless nights spent in similar positions, listening to Michael snoring, feeling stuck. Feeling like she couldn't change her life. Now she tries to live spontaneously; she never wants to trap herself again. So she makes an excuse and dresses, says she has to feed her dog.

'But I had big plans for breakfast,' he says. 'Eggs, juice, maybe a back rub.'

'Aww, that sounds great but—'

'Promise you'll text me?'

His desperation's weird, but there is something sweet about him, almost boyish. It must be those quick, animated eyes. 'Maybe I'll see you,' she says gently, closing his bedroom door.

In the taxi on the way home, she experiences a sudden, powerful desire to call her ex.

'What's the matter, are you okay?'

'What went wrong between us, Mick? I feel as though I can't remember. But there must have been something.'

'Is that why you called? Joy, it's four in the morning; I thought something had gone wrong. Where have you been?'

'I was so unhappy. I thought nothing good would ever happen to me again.'

'Can we talk about this another time?'

'Do you think it's because after Frida, we couldn't have another baby?'

'No, I don't.'

'What then?'

'Honestly, Joy? I thought you knew. I'm not the one who wanted it to end.'

THE NEXT MORNING JOY wakes feeling worse than ever. She always feels a little shameful when she wakes up with a hangover, and then she remembers calling Michael at 4 a.m. Lying there, smelling like sex and stale wine, she chastises herself for acting like a teenager. She sends him an apology and then, too guilty to stay in bed, downs a couple of painkillers and a Hydralyte, showers, drags on runners and a raincoat and heads outside to walk the dog.

It is drizzling, humid. For a Saturday there's hardly anyone around. Joy walks to the oval, feeling better with every step. After last night her body is sensitive to the air, the humidity, the fabric of her clothes. She feels strangely awake. Near a group of warehouses, the air is toasty with the smell of roasting coffee. Her dog frolics in the wet. In the daylight she is able to get her bearings; she's not a hundred per cent sure, but she thinks the younger man's house is nearby. If she hung a right and walked for ten minutes in the direction of the city, she'd arrive outside his door.

Her phone chimes with a text message from an unknown number. It's him, saying he had a great time last night and can he have her email. Her email? It's a strange request but it can't hurt. Seconds later, her phone makes the swooshing sound to indicate an email has come through. The subject simply reads, *Proposal*. Involuntarily, she thinks of the time Michael asked her to marry him and she said no. Well, for a while she said yes, but then a couple of months before the wedding, Joy imagined standing at the altar and realised that she couldn't promise, before all their family and friends, to cherish Michael until one or other of their deaths. It just wasn't possible. Who could, in good faith, make a promise like that? Not that she didn't love him. She just wasn't sure she'd love him always.

The proposal in the email does not pertain to marriage but contains an employment opportunity which might interest her. The younger man recalls Joy telling him she is looking for work and coincidentally he is looking for someone to perform a cash job. He's got all the info if she wants it. Short-term, with the possibility to extend.

Joy is intrigued. She wonders why he's being generous; he must have really liked her. Maybe there's a red light flashing in her brain, telling her not to mix business with pleasure, but either she ignores it or she doesn't notice. *If you're keen to have a chat about the job*, he writes, *here is my address*. It feels as though the universe is telling her to see him one more time. So she walks home, dries the dog off with a towel, packs his food and drops him at her sister's.

'Are you going away or something?' asks her sister, holding the dog by his collar so he doesn't follow Joy back to the car.

'Maybe,' says Joy smiling, leaning against the door.

'Oh my God – you've met someone, haven't you?'

'Maybe, baby,' she repeats mysteriously, leaping into the car and driving off.

She feels possessed of a sudden vitality. Fuck Pilates – she feels like she could climb a mountain. She could swim the Bass Strait, pump iron, go on a bender, fuck a rugby team.

Maybe not that far.

But fuck it, Joy feels good.

The man's house is gorgeous, an Edwardian weatherboard with cast iron latticework and a sprawling, shady garden through which the rain drips oh so sweetly. She knocks on the door and he opens it immediately, as if he has been standing there waiting for her all this time. They look at each other and the attraction from last night sparks up again and quivers like a naked flame between them.

'Hi,' he says, extending a hand. 'I'm Doogz Dermody. I didn't catch your name.'

'Joy,' she says, 'just ... Joy!'

'Perfect,' he smiles, beckoning her inside.

In the kitchen Doogz offers to make her a green juice. It's not really her thing but before she can protest he begins drawing fruit and vegetables from the crisper: celery, apple, avocado, kale, some seaweed powder called spirulina which was popular in the nineties. 'I don't know what it is, but being around you makes me feel invigorated,' he yells above the turbine. 'I haven't felt this way in ages!'

Joy can hardly hear him but she thinks he follows it with, *I've never met anyone like you,* even though what she actually hears is something like, 'anemone monkey-fun haiku.'

It doesn't matter. She feels it too.

He hands her a tall glass and kisses her hard on the mouth. She can feel his teeth through his lips and taste the juice on him, the chlorophyllic sweetness and the hygienic language of self-improvement. When he lets her go, she feels dazed. He leads her back down the hallway into a series of interconnected rooms where the walls appear to be covered in empty egg cartons. 'Soundproofing,' Doogz clarifies. 'Good for when we have rehearsals. This way, we can play as loud as we want and the neighbours won't hear a thing.'

He bids her take a seat on a low red couch and perches opposite her on a high stool, where he begins to speak of the uncommon gastrointestinal condition he has which causes inflammation of the gut, chronic fatigue, anxiety and depression. It has a devastating effect on his music; he is often too sick to go on tour, his faculties are dulled, sometimes he goes to play guitar and his entire hand seizes up. Thankfully, he was able to participate in a clinical trial where he learned to perform a procedure called a *faecal microbiota transplant* (FMT) on himself. The trial changed his life. A daily dose of good poo, he says, is his only chance at feeling normal.

Joy fingers the dials on a mixing desk absent-mindedly, but now Doogz snaps at her, 'Don't touch that!'

'Oh shit. Sorry! I didn't even realise.'

'Fucking hell,' he says, leaping up and making some adjustments to the dials. 'You've changed all the levels. I'm going to have to do it over before the next rehearsal. Fuck.'

'I'm so sorry,' says Joy.

'No, no, it's fine. Don't apologise. These things happen.' Regaining his composure, he resumes his speech from before. Since the trial, he's implemented a system for treating the disease from home. All he needs is a donor, some saline solution, a working freezer and an enema bag.

'I'm not sure that I follow,' says Joy.

'Aha!' he exclaims, leaning forward so that his face is very close to hers. 'She's not sure that she follows! Let me enlighten you, Joy.' A beam of light struggles through a gap in the studio curtains, searing a diagonal stripe across his face, and in this attitude Doogz Dermody looks like a backyard prophet, luminous and deranged, and Joy is suffused with an acute religious feeling. She cannot help thinking this is one of those times where it is okay, essential even, to eschew normal logic, like during wartime, or when people are falling in love.

Doogz is looking at her deeply. He has stopped moving and now sits completely still. It's very affecting. In this taut atmosphere, Joy finds herself leaning forward, wanting to answer a question his body seems to ask of hers.

'I'm still not sure what you're asking.'

'I've been looking for someone I can trust,' he says. 'I know it's crazy – we've only just met. But I feel like you're that person.'

'You want me to be your donor? But you don't even know me. Don't you need to test me or something, to see if I'm … I don't know, healthy?'

'My mother always said I was very intuitive Joy, ever since I was a child. We can talk about tests, contracts, all those details later. There's something about you. I can tell that you're exactly what I need.'

Joy thinks it's a risky kind of science, but she likes being swept up in his fervour. 'Just so we're clear … you're asking me to donate my poo to you on a regular basis, in return for a cash payment, so that you can take my shit with you on tour?'

'Do you want to see how it works?'

Joy doesn't say yes or no but simply follows, as if there's a length of rope connecting her to Doogz. She recalls a holiday she and Michael took to New Zealand in the noughties, so that he could buy this special guitar from a man in the Waitākere Mountains, west of Auckland. On a spare day they tried to bungee jump in tandem, but at the last minute Michael had a panic attack and didn't want to go. She rubbed his back and soothed him, waiting for his panic to subside, feeling both magnanimous and resentful, for she had spent many hours at the guitar maker's little factory, tailing the men as they talked gear and tools and types of trees, and this was supposed to be her treat.

'Have you ever bungee jumped before?' she asks Doogz.

'I have actually. It was fucking awesome.'

With Doogz now there is this crazy lightness, this unfathomable drop. Forget extreme sports – she has never liked a feeling more.

DOOGZ TAKES HER TO a laundry he has kitted out as a makeshift laboratory. He opens a big chest freezer and withdraws what looks to be a takeaway container: this is the *faecal storage unit* (FSU). Joy peers inside the freezer and counts the units; there is only one left, which means that he's run out. He opens the FSU and there's a frozen turd inside. 'My last donor quit on me. Says he couldn't handle the pressure.' Doogz sounds disappointed, like he thinks the guy was weak.

Now it's time to homogenise the donation in a blender with some saline solution before pouring the liquid into an enema bag using a sieve to rid the mix of any lumps. Joy watches, disturbed but mesmerised, like when you see a commuter picking earwax on the tram, or an animal with its penis out. Doogz chats the whole time, which makes the situation feel more normal. He talks about the weather, about gigs, about the people in his band. He does not make jokes or take the piss, sticking instead to the euphemistic language of science: *stool, procedure, FMT.*

When transferring the mix to the enema bag he refers to the substance, enigmatically, as *THE SOLUTION.*

When the bag is nice and full, Doogz takes off his pants behind a plastic shower curtain patterned with monstera leaves. Joy contemplates the pattern idly, listening as Doogz tells her that he always administers the FMT himself. Afterward, he lies on his back while the solution works its magic. They chat about the wonders of little and large things, as if their work does not reveal the sordid excretions of the body, but nothing less than movements of the soul.

WHEN IT IS DONE, Doogz takes a shower. He bids her wait in the loungeroom, where she sinks into another couch. Saturday afternoon is waning. She slips off her shoes and rests her feet on the coffee table, pleased there's nowhere else she needs to be. It occurs to her that she is having a bizarre experience, but at the same time it feels normal, like she has done it all before.

Doogz appears before her wrapped in just a towel. From her seated position Joy presses her face into his crotch, rubbing it back and forth across the damp fabric until she feels him get excited. It's so easy, she thinks with pleasure – he has the advantage of being young.

They do it on the couch. It's different this time, maybe because it's afternoon or because Joy has been initiated into Doogz's peculiar world. He is even more passionate than he was last night – she wants to say *unleashed*. The eye contact is back and he is trying hard, so hard that Joy feels as though he's less making love to her than plundering her depths; it's so intense and overwhelming that she almost wants to cry, although she doesn't know what she's crying for, and so, embarrassed, she crushes her face into the couch.

Night drops in like a welcome guest. He lights some candles and turns on a lamp, and in the mild glow she feels as though she's walked outside her life and into someone else's. Doogz is a complex mix of sensitivity and arrogance, easiness and pain. She realises this is something she's attracted to in men, the tortured artist type. She thought she was over this since Michael, but perhaps these things are hard to shake.

For dinner he prepares something vegetarian and elaborate, and she notes wryly that the shelf in his kitchen is stacked with every single Ottolenghi book. The food is okay but kind of tasteless. He pours them each a sparkling water and she asks if she should nick out to get some wine.

'I don't drink,' he says.

'Really? What about last night?'

'Non-alcoholic, baby! There's some decent stuff out there these days.' He looks at her admiringly. 'Besides, I feel so god in your company that drinking would just ruin it.'

'Did you just say *God*?'

'Good, I said good. I feel good when I'm around you. But maybe you make me feel invincible too, like a kind of god.'

'Um,' says Joy. 'Thanks ... ?' She could really do with the wine.

After dinner Doogz plays some records and they wind around each other on the couch, talking about everything – their lives, their careers, their parents. Joy tells him her mother died of cancer and her father's become a recluse, hardly daring to see anyone, letting his house fall down around him. Doogz tries to sympathise. 'I don't talk to my dad anymore,' he says, and Joy has the tact not to press. But his mother is alive and well in Toorak, and the way he talks about her makes Joy think he's used to playing down his family's wealth.

'So you went to a private school?' she asks him.

'Yeah, in Geelong. From Year 9 upwards.'

'Why not the whole time?'

'My parents only sent me there after, well ... it's difficult to explain. Basically my parents split, Dad ran off with some bitch he met at work and Mum was really lonely, so for a while I was, you know, like sleeping in her bed. Nothing weird happened, but Dad came over one afternoon to pick me up for band rehearsal or something and

Mum was depressed and I think maybe she was naked, or I was – something like that. Dad flipped out. Sent me to boarding school.'

Joy does not know what to do with this information. She likes to be open-minded, but it is all a little weird.

'So ...' he asks after a pause. 'You never gave me an answer.'

Relieved by the change of subject she asks, 'About what?'

'About the job, being my donor. I have a gig tomorrow night and as you may have noticed, I'm running low on supplies.'

'Oh,' she begins, 'I don't know ...'

'It's no big deal,' says Doogz, stroking her arm. He bites the side of her neck gently and then deeply, baring his teeth. Joy squirms and tries to wriggle from his grasp, but he holds her firmly until she stops.

'What was that about?'

'I'll pay you, obviously,' he says.

Joy sits up and rubs her neck. 'I'm not sure about this Doogz. I feel like we're really connecting, and I don't think it's a good idea to bring money into it.'

'Listen, I really need this. I'm not asking much. Why do you think I went through all of that stuff in the laundry?'

'I don't know. Aren't I too old? What's the recommended age for a faecal donor?'

'Come on, it's not like you're an ancient old lady.'

'I'm fifty-five.'

Doogz looks momentarily stunned. 'Oh ... I thought you were younger. Not that it matters. Yeah—' he says, recovering, 'yeah, the recommended window for donors is between the ages of eighteen and fifty. But that's just a guideline. You seem fit so you've probably got a few good years in you yet.'

'You make me sound like ... I dunno, a breeder's bitch or something.'

'Sorry, sorry. I mean that you're probably quite healthy, as far as your microbiome goes. Usually we would do an extensive range of tests, but desperate times call for desperate measures. It's just a once-off until we can get a formal process going.'

Joy reiterates that she doesn't see this being a good idea. 'It's like the old saying – *don't shit where you eat.*'

Doogz's face darkens, an expression Joy recognises from when she came upon him on the staircase. 'Whatever,' he says. 'Stupid cunt.'

Shaken, Joy gets up and starts looking for her things as Doogz starts pleading with her. 'Don't go,' he wheedles, 'I'm so, so sorry. Wow. That was so unlike me, I never lose my temper and I don't often use that word. Seriously, I totally respect your choice not to get involved. I guess I'm just getting desperate. If I don't get another sample for tomorrow I'm going to be completely fucked.'

'It must be hard,' says Joy carefully. She is beginning to feel – she doesn't want to think it, but there it is – a little scared.

'Yeah, it's not your problem. Don't worry. I'll sort it out.'
He comes over and puts his arms around her, but Joy does
not want to be cuddled anymore.

'Anyway,' she says, extracting herself, 'I think it's time for
me to go. Thanks for dinner and … yeah. It was really nice.'

'Oh God.' Doogz throws himself onto the couch in
exaggerated despair. 'I've scared you off, haven't I?' He puts
his head in his hands and looks as if he is about to weep.
'My whole life, people have been afraid of my emotions.
I'm highly expressive and it puts people off. It's just … I feel
things so deeply! I sometimes wonder if I'll ever find
someone who gets me.'

'Don't be like that,' says Joy. 'I had a lovely time. I just
need to get home.'

'Please don't go.'

'Well it's just … I need to feed my dog.'

'That's what you said last night! Who has the dog? Can't
they feed him?'

'Yeah, well, that's what happens when you have an animal.
You have to look after it.'

'Who's going to look after me?'

It's pathetic, but she feels bad for him. The fear has
dulled and she cannot be bothered resisting any longer.
A wave of pure fatigue breaks over her. 'Okay,' she says,
'I'll stay.'

'Yay!' he brightens. 'I knew you would.'

Before they go to bed, Doogz prepares some kind of
herbal tea which quickly makes her drowsy. He takes her to

his bed and tucks her in gently, tenderly, as if it's Joy who's now the child. Her sleep is total, dreamless, but at one point she thinks she wakes and Doogz is kneeling over her, naked, breathing very close to her face. Fretfully she rolls from under him, settles and goes back to sleep. In the morning she is groggy, can't tell where she has been.

'What the hell was in that tea...' she starts to ask him, realising he is not in bed with her. It feels late; she wants to check the time but her phone's not where she left it. Neither are her keys, her wallet, she can't remember if she even brought a bag. It's impossible to think. She hears the sound of pots and pans, the cutlery drawer opening and closing, water gushing out the tap. It is Sunday and the radio is on, she recognises the presenter, it's the same show she listens to at home, *Kick-Ons with Larry*. The presenter is reading off the list of subscribers and he finishes by giving a massive shout-out to a new subscriber, Joy from Northcote, thanks a lot.

'I subscribed you to my favourite station,' he says, coming into the bedroom with some breakfast on a tray. 'Those guys have been absolute legends backing my music from day one and I just thought, hey, Joy's going to be sticking around here for a while – may as well get her on the team.'

Actually she has to go, she tells him – she's stayed too long already. Plus she needs to pick the dog up from her sister's before midday. 'Aww, poochy again. Don't worry about him,' says Doogz soothingly, 'we'll think about all that stuff once you've eaten breakfast.'

What is happening? Joy watches him take a spoon from the tray and dip it into a bowl of chia porridge. He begins to feed her, spooning the healthy slop into her mouth. She swallows obediently. They are silent until it's over and Doogz sets the bowl back on the tray.

'Now it's time to get you clean,' he says, pulling her out of bed. He marshals her into the bathroom and turns on the shower. The water is hot and raises goosebumps on Joy's skin. 'You're going to love the gig tonight. We've got the whole band doing an epic set. Great supports. I think it's going to be a vibe.'

He strips off too and enters the cubicle. There is hardly any room but Doogz takes the soap and begins to wash her, rubbing her arms and shoulders, her breasts and belly, her legs, even between her toes, massaging her skin in firm, soapy circles, working up a lather. When he gets to her vulva he inserts a single finger, pushing it deep inside her before removing it again. Joy does not know why he does it; his dick's not even hard. It's worse than if it was. She goes rigid, like she will shatter if he touches her again. She is cold. The water misses her and clatters to the floor.

Shampooing her hair, he says, 'God, look at you. You're in such good condition for a woman your age, I can't believe I didn't realise you were over fifty. That's like, as old as my mother. Does that get you off, knowing you could be my mother?'

Joy does not reply. When she is completely soapy Doogz turns her around beneath the rushing faucet, rinsing her clean. As she is turning, Joy closes her eyes and feels that same sensation from yesterday, the awful lightness.

He towels her off and lets her dress. The breakfast things look sorry from their tray and Joy pulls clothes on frantically, not knowing whether they are inside out, rushing to escape. Yet before she has her shoes on, Doogz returns with another juice.

'Here, I made you a good one.'

'No thanks … I'm full of chia.'

Her nervous laugh.

'Trust me, you're going to want to taste this,' he insists.

'No thanks, really. I should get going.'

'You're telling me you don't have time for this *piece of art*? Look – it's got apple, pear, mint, ginger, the works. Here—' He holds the glass out for her. 'Take it.'

'I really don't—'

'*Take it.*'

Joy takes the glass and sips.

'You're going to want the whole thing,' says Doogz. 'Drink it all up … that's good, just like that.'

She holds her breath and gulps until the glass is empty. Outwardly she's calm, but her mind goes through scenarios she has seen in films, it goes out to her sister, her daughter, her dog, even Michael. She wonders where she can get a hold of someone's phone, should she call the police, if she screams will anyone hear her, but of course the place is soundproofed; *this way the neighbours won't hear a thing.* The juice tastes a bit weird but if she can just get it down maybe he will leave her for a minute and she'll have time to run away.

'There's a good girl,' says Doogz sweetly. 'See, it wasn't that hard.'

Joy stands, preparing to disappear. 'Thanks, no, that was really wonderful. Aren't you going to put that in the dishwasher?'

'No, I think I'll hang onto it for a while. So … what do you want to do today? I'm thinking we get cosy, watch a movie on the couch. God,' he reaches for her, 'I can't get enough of you. You're just so … yummy.'

Her skin crawls. She feels violently ill, doubling over like someone has squeezed her gut in a vice. She runs to the toilet, clutching her stomach.

'Don't flush, okay?' Doogz calls out behind her. 'We're running on tank water.'

Hardly unbuckling her jeans in time, Joy sinks onto the toilet seat and sweats until it is done. Dimly, she registers no sound when it falls into the bowl – a phantom – but she is too relieved to care.

When she goes to flush she finds the button on the cistern has been covered up with masking tape. In the bowl her poo is suspended at an invisible threshold, and it takes a few seconds to realise that Doogz has stretched a sheet of plastic wrap beneath the seat. The door cracks open and he's there.

'Remember not to flush,' he says, his eyes bright again and snarling.

'What have you done?' asks Joy.

In his hand is a clean faecal storage unit. 'Desperate times,' says Doogz, shoving her out of his way.

NEW DIRECTIONS

WEST: Animal voices are annoying, says my writer friend,
stirring sugar into her tea. She has stopped drinking coffee because it makes her feel uneasy. I ask
her what she means. Eco fiction is trending, she
says, but that doesn't mean it's good. I've met her
in a café west of the city, something we do peri-
odically to exchange ideas, by which of course
we mean to bitch about the opportunities we've
missed and all the people who've surpassed us.
Past us, beyond the premises it's raining, a grimy
rain which smears pollutants over windscreens,
under awnings and down drains. I say that I've
been feeling under the weather lately, depressed
by all life's grime. Life's got us by the gonads,
she replies, plundering the depths of her tote bag

and then mine. She scrabbles around, takes out a book – here, she says, look: basically, a global pandemic spawns a preternatural reaction; suddenly, the people who've had this strange disease understand the speech of beasts. I wish I thought of that, I say. There's nothing to it, she dismisses. Then we leave the café. Outside, I ask her if she thinks it's really all that easy. My friend eyes me suspiciously.

Don't get any ideas.

NORTH: I've developed a remedy for writer's block. Lately I have taken to imagining a string of random associations starting with an object on my desk. I cast about for something to hold onto and my eyes wrap round a lighting cable: the braided wire in its shiny Kevlar casing makes me think of scales, slipperiness, eels. Years ago I underwent a spell of psychoanalysis during which I had recurring dreams of blindness; either my eyes wouldn't open due to some horrific illness or impairment, or it would be imperative for me to perform impossible tasks – skiing, computer graphics, acrobatics – with them closed. I remember telling my analyst that the dreams made me feel like an eel and that the feeling of eelness was connected to knowledge and to a sense of longing. This is important, said my analyst. This question of desire. Opening

my browser I search for eels, turning up an article from 2015 reporting that marine biologists
in London were concerned that local European
eels were hyperactive due to the amount of trace
cocaine polluting the River Thames. The drug
had a devastating effect on the eels' sympathetic
nervous systems, thus disturbing their hormones
thus arresting their development thus preventing
them from reaching sexual maturity thus contrib-
uting to species loss. I feel strangely excited by this
absurd chain of cause and effect and

that is when I have an idea.

SOUTH: A short-finned eel is discovered in a south-facing
water feature at the university where I sometimes
teach. I hear the story in a roundabout way and
doubt whether it is true, for it has the magic and
strangeness of myth. The man who discovered it,
a professor of architecture, becomes obsessed with
its origin story. He consults a group of Wurund-
jeri elders, who yarn about a vast network of
billabongs and freshwater streams which used to
be important migratory paths for short-finned
eels. The university was built atop a superhighway!
The campus grew, and as it grew these ancient
waterways were pushed underground, dammed,
redirected, contained in stormwater drains ...

But the water still flows.

EAST: miriamwebster_92@gmail.com
From: submissions@theeasternreview.com.au
         Thank you for pitching your idea for a short fic-
         tion piece titled 'The Slip.' We think it would be
         a great fit for The Eastern Review's forthcoming
         issue, 'New Directions in Anthropomorphism.'
         Please send your final draft by the end of the
         month and we will get stuck into editing.
                         P.S. Great idea. Why the eel?

*   *   *

THE SLIP

A woman comes to my clinic after the death of her sister.
I ask how she occupies herself; she says she works in zoologi-
cal research at the university, developing a breeding program
for short-finned eels. I have never seen a short-finned eel and
I am not sure that I'd like to. I ask when her sister died; she
says last April. I note it's now early March, that almost a
year has passed. I ask her sister's name; she says Anna. She
is reticent on all subjects but her eels. Before she leaves, she
recounts a recurring dream in which she is herself an eel.
This piques my interest. How does it feel to be an eel? *It feels
like a question without an*

answer, and I wake thinking there is something I should know. In my first session, I feel as though I'm doing it all wrong. The analyst looks exactly like you think she would. It's clear I should be talking about Anna but why am I talking about eels? I tell her about the glass eels I am raising, each one as long as my little finger and completely transparent, flickering in the green water of the hatchling tanks, catching light like flashing jewels.

The night before my second session I dream again of

yeah body. eel body. dream body, covert like a line redacted. unreliable archive. a paradox, body constituted by those organs that it lacks. lack like punctuation indicates a [   ].

body like a question mark or comma, all that's enigmatic in your language. wide open to inquiry but to all examinations lidded heavily. an eye. a box. an eye peering through the key-hole. I want to be reckoned with on my own terms and energies. yeah. body yeah yeah. we should go somewhere together where we've never been before. the body knows the way although it's true that intuition is a slippery bitch   the
                                             river in this
                                        city is narcotic
                                                     bliss

and all the
eels are ~~fucking~~
getting high.

I used to be a nice eel but now I'm a poet I'm hysterical I writhe and glimmer and speed through
the river like gossip. I'm high on shit cocaine and
all the other eels I know are getting blind. I'm
longing for salt water, feel more slippery than ever,
need a circuit breaker, salty taste to rid myself of
city smells. Enough of these narcotics. If you're
worried about a speaking eel rest assured I won't
be signifying it like this or only here and there.
Reckon it's annoying? Reckon you're the only one

Getting used to how this works? Just keep speaking, I urge.
Let yourself

hear the word eel in feelings ... Isn't that strange?
There's something inside these little guys that makes
them want to go deeper. Once they've lived for twenty
years they stop eating and swim toward the sea without
quite knowing why. Did you know that eels spawn once
and then they die? There's something literary about it,
no? Something about coming full circle, about birth as
an encounter with death, and death with birth; something about a life's purpose, something about a quest ...

Am I right in saying that

the eels are disappearing. I wasn't always interested in eels, but I fell in love with them like falling under an enchantment. My sister used to joke about it: you're a sick fish, she would say. Overfishing is one thing, but otherwise we can't explain it. I'm inclined to think they're leaving because we've done something to make them go away. It grieves me. I feel I'm chasing after ghosts. It would be easier to be uncaring, but that would be a waste of good

feelings are for humans and other social animals. I've got a boner for being a-loner / and I like it that way

Go on

okay
I lied. I don't even have them yet –
sex organs I mean.
(they're coming)
(cumming)
haha
My body is its own intractable poetry.

Drugs can change you if you like. When you think about it, we're all a bunch of chemicals

swimming round inside a skin sack filled with
water, meat and other crap. The river's murky
'cause of all the rain. I'm open to pretty much
anything, like rubbish washing in. Like low
light, low visibility, high pollution makes me
f r e a k   y. For a while I was getting high with
this couple called Nikki and Brendan; Nikki
was a sweetie but Brendan bloody Brendan no
you wouldn't find a slipperier fuckwit in the
entire order of Anguilliformes worse than a
Moray and believe me those Morays can be super
fucking cunty anyway that's beside the point

so

one night we're floating round our usual spot
gills open mainlining hits directly from the
pipe when I get this sudden wild murmur it
starts in my anal fin and then goes dorsal, then
it's in my head my neck my gills the freaky sib-
ilance the fuck is this some really good gear or
what? the uncontrollable urge to start swimming for the   ocean
    It's VERY sexual Brendan's like fuck man ...

NOT YOU TOO!!!!????

– but I'm off like a hard clam spat from
the mouth of an irate cormorant.

Question: *Are you apprehensive about the
mass spawning event you're headed for,
where every eel on the continent will meet
under a golden rainforest of seaweed and
spill themselves with abandon through the
salty, burning blue?*

A: I've never done anything like that before but I
never say never. The Naturalists worked out long
ago that eels spawn once and then they die. The
Naturalists got a lot out of this and wrote many
books, but all I got was a tender promise which
happened also to be a death sentence …

But fuck it, you know, you only spawn

once in the Spring of 1876, a young Sigmund Freud spent
a month in Trieste dissecting eels. I mention this to my
analysand, who is unfamiliar with the story. Freud wished
to locate the eel's gonads and thereby solve the question
of its nativity, but the eel proved slippery, unsolvable, and
Freud turned his mind to psychoanalysis, that other sliding

thing the young scientist never understood was that the
ones he was studying weren't the right sort of eels. They

were too young; their gonads hadn't formed. It is only during the long migration to sea that the eel's stomach dissolves and sex organs grow in its place. Still, scientists are not quite sure how exactly eels reproduce. I'm attracted to their secrets, our failure to know them. Even if my research comes to nothing, I will be a witness to their extinction. I think it's important. I did not see my sister die, which I experience as a failure. Anna's death could have been many things – a sense of an ending, a spiritual requirement, a catalyst, a question, a moment of peace. I will never know. I think my dream about the eel is related to this

sense that life is short! I'm swimming faster and faster into the arms of fate and it's kind of funny because I know I'm headed for my own funeral. At the start of my journey I was feeling really ~~wired wierd~~ wreid ~~we ird~~ fuck's sake WEIRD; being in clear water for the first time had me feeling kind of toxic

(sullied base defiled infected polluted ruined corrupt marred foul).

Contrast: the great illuminator!

When I think about it (and I've had a lot of time to think about it), feeling like a butcher's arsehole probably had a lot to do with getting clean. I don't just mean the improvement in water quality but

com in   g

down from all that coke.

Sorry about the eel voice but it's like the further I get from where I've been the less oppressive your diction feels. If you wanted a story in which the animals speak perfect fucking English then you're reading the wrong

stories are never benign descriptions and speech – talking as well as listening – opens up the possibility for both the speaker and the hearer to be transformed. I think the woman knows this. Certainly, that's why we're here. She tells me that the eel-dream feels like longing; but for what, she is uncertain. *This is important,* I say. *This question of desire.*

Lately she's preoccupied with arranging sexual encounters via dating apps. When I press her, she changes the subject, tells me about another dream in which she is

the young Freud in Trieste. I see shimmering dead tissue, his hands stained by the white and red blood of marine animals, cell detritus swimming before my eyes. Black bodies, writhing. His hands, writing. Taking notes. The room is dim, the inside smells of the sea and death and I work at a desk in the corner, slicing my charges. Their writhing disturbs me. Like a hysteric the eel invites and then repels me. It will not be managed. It refuses to be known.

I am the young scientist in a foreign country in a strange city in a dark room. I am the hunter, prowling the creature for meaning but it does not come. I flee into the night and go down, down, down toward the pier. I watch the fishermen hauling in the evening catch, see bodies slick with sand and scale, see tentacles, see fins and gills and beaks. See mouths. See the women taking air, strolling, fixing their dresses, their hair. Beauties, all of them, beguiling and strange, but no more intriguing than my eels. I see my hands, bloody. My hands, writing. On the desk there is a letter addressed to my friend. I open it to see what I have written. *Trieste is a very beautiful city*, it reads, *its beasts are very beautiful beasts!*

When I wake I don't know what led me to imagine

the carnage. You think just because I'm an elongated aquatic vertebrate who moves by generating waves along my slender body that I can't put myself in the big man's shoes? You want me to make a SCENE? Here's a fucking scene:

he pauses in his work to slip the letter in his
pocket. *I shan't write separately to you on how
I eat, drink, spend my days. I'd rather report on
what I've seen of la bella Italia and how I go with
the beast killing science.* The beast killing science!
What a load of

e x c r e m e n t
                        wonder why he goes to
                        the port at
                        sunset
                        the fucking little

creep perving on those ladies pathologising
frowns and sighs and catching handkerchiefs
and treading on the trains of dresses in his haste
to sniff their hair – hair sniffing is a disgusting
trait of mammals, by the way. The sun drops
then it dips its bloody rag into the ocean so the
ocean seems like it's on fire. The young scientist
calls us sea creatures even though we're creatures
of both places, sea and river, shiver between
                                        worlds
straddling boundaries sometimes
walking on our fins no
writhing body patterned
sequences of syllables
too evolved to

shiver shifty and too
shifting, too unbounded for
the likes of
you.

Like I said to an oystercatcher once:
Deal with it, mothershucker.

Back to Freud or should we call him Sigi there
is something niggling and unruly in this foreign
twilight collar turns his hair blown quickly by a
sneaky little seabreeze. Snatches of talk on the
wind. Littoral messages. Associative shoreline.
Lace coral. Shell shock. Electric current. Bright
eddy. Pearl earring with a matching choker. Jok-
ing – hiding smiles behind gloved flippers. Feels
pointed. He longs to approach the ladies on the
promenade, though what he desires he cannot
say. On these evenings he scurries past, afraid of
himself, returning to his eels.

*The sea, which may be seen at all times from my
window, is usually as smooth as glass.* Some folks
say obsession is the highest form of flattery but
in my opinion that is kind of maladjusted. Oh
but Sigi's just a boy, a man-child flirting with
the point of individuation, addicted to the killing *which disturbs me even in my dreams, in my*

thoughts nothing but the great problems connected
with the words ducts, testicles *and* ovaries, *uni-*
versal words and

nothing but the

BIG QUESTIONS

the ones that go hand in hole with

gonads!

gonads!

gonads – the universal,

pivotal questions. We try to interpret this dream about
Freud. The woman says she has made a career researching
unusual creatures but grief is an animal stranger than most.
Sometimes it is tight and small and particular, but at others
she suspects this mournfulness is shared by many, so there
is consolation in knowing that she does not suffer it alone.
She asks: could what we are doing here be a way to trace her
survival? I sense that something has

shifted, apparently, although I don't feel like I'm making any steps toward a cure. I'm just lying on the couch
about to burst with talk I cannot bring myself to utter.

With the men my reticence is never a problem; if you let them, most prefer to speak about themselves. My mother keeps calling in the middle of the night, she's worried about me, she can't get the time difference right. I don't want to talk about Anna and sex is a good distraction. I like the sweating writhing grinding. I like binding my body with others. Afterward, when my partner is sleeping and I am cool and quiet, my thoughts return to eels. My hatchlings are growing now, losing their translucence, becoming creatures of substance. In the early hours of the morning I leave whatever bed I'm in and head to the lab, where I stand before their tanks and watch the eels swim through my reflection, blurring my edges before

       filling page after page with * insert picture here *
       our reproductive systems though he doesn't
       know exactly how to draw it. If the boy-man
       knows already what he'll know once he is older
       it's that every patient *yields to the compulsion to*
       repeat and in such cases where the resistance is
       greater the repetition will be gonads

       gonads

       too. He breaks for a coffee – perhaps he takes
       two sugars, stirs thrice – before returning to
       his microscope to peer at slides which frame

the slick remains of my great-great-great-great-
great-great-great-great-great-great-great-great-
great-great-great-great-great-great-great-great-
great-grandmother like stills from a slasher
film I like to think it was my grandma anyway
and not just an eelstress who happened to look
exactly like her like to think of him in crisis: crisis of science, crisis of self, crisis of image blurred
* he focuses the lens * still blurry, not like me,
streaming toward the sea with this sudden clarity
of vision.

I feel ethereal!

At first it really fucked with me, with my sense
of having a soul or spirit or whatever; I guess
it's normal for earthbound creatures to cling to
feelings of embodiment. It is the strangest thing
to seek your own annihilation. A terrific pressure builds inside me. I think it means I need to
hurry. Can't get mired in any ocean gyres and
find that I've arrived

late, being evasive. In secret, I find it intolerable. In session,
I say LISTEN: either you want to be here doing the work,
or you don't. She surprises me by failing to appear for her
last session before the Christmas break. So, she's given me
the slip. That week I dream that there's a wave, a big wave

coming to wipe everything and everybody out. In the dream
a panel of advisors asks *Why don't you listen when your own
life is at*

stakes are high for me right now, alone in my apartment while the rest of the world's on holiday. I refused
to fly home and see my mother. I couldn't bear the
heat, the sun, the ham, the brandy without Anna. This
foreign climate keeps the memory on ice and I keep
lights off and the curtains closed. About a week ago I
dreamed I was an eel again. As the migrating eel gets
closer to the sea, its eyes widen and turn blue in order
to absorb light underwater, but in the dream my eyes
don't clear and I can't find my way. Since then I've
been losing sight in my left eye, like there's an ink blot
over my iris. I haven't seen any doctors but I've been
Googling it and think it must be an ocular occlusion,
probably due to psychic distress.

(I know what you're thinking. My analyst is going to

have fun with this, bitch!! I've been feeling philosophically minded on this last leg of
the journey, like that cunt Rousseau ... or is
it Cousteau? Which one's the shark guy and
which one's the frog? It's hard to tell with these
Enlightenment types. For one thing they're
all named Jacques, a name I hate by the way.

You didn't ask but here's a compendium of my friends' monikers: Nikki, Brendan, Libramax, Dettol, Batshit, Common Dog Winkle, Sammy, Glasgow, Hans the Shoveller, Curly, Barry the Crab (he's actually a limpet, don't ask), Mernda, Bonbeach, Ativan, Lifestyles Extra Large, Constance, Cool Climate Chardonnay and Flux. Guess I'll never be seeing that fine crew of urchins, con artists and guttersnipes again! Fuck me sideways, or should I say fuck me dead. Because it strikes me that it's coming. I try to let these words sink in, but the closer I get to where I'm going the more my sense of fatalism warps and bends into an idea – and I'm wary of sounding overly redemptive here – of freedom.

But sea here see inside her I'm embarrassed to admit that for all my pompous airs I'm still like the sweating writhing grinding stranger than most   almost old   no hold on it's hold, holdtight

    want   some seafood?   Now is not the time for song and dance, dickhead! Now's the moment for some eleventh-hour reflections on BEING and

time has a different texture when you can't observe its
passing. I wear an eyepatch – I know – and lose the
ability to judge distance. Some eels take up to a year to
migrate depending on currents, place of origin, vigour
and inclination. They are blind for most of the way, getting by on feeling. Maybe this is a lesson. See feelingly, say
the eels. I think about this for a few days, grappling with

       so many sensations!!
             salty   warm
        blue   delirious   yellowbrown
seaweed everywhere like a beautiful golden
fuck-palace. Eels everywhere, fucking. Well not
fucking, spawning, but that's how I have to put
it so I'm speaking a language we all understand.
So, we're all here spawning/fucking every which
way. Upside down around sideways lots of hand
in holes tell me the hole truth and nothing but
the truth so help you Cod oh baby baby lots of
places to enter lots of places to return *Either you
want to be here doing the work or* fuck yeah I
fucking want to be here sure as waves caress the
sea and gods fuck mortal sluts and wicked mer-
maids tell sweet fibs and currents have no motive
and the temperatures are rising and the rubbish
is collecting and the crabs have no compunction
and the kelp is all aflutter and the images are
burning and the scriptures do not alter and the

story is irrelevant and the truth is worse than it
appeared at first and science is a fiction and conspiracies are coded and my organs disappeared to
let the gonad sing a round and even if you don't
believe it every starfish is a swine (this is something you would know if you had seen one send
its stomach on reconnaissance, blindly tonguing
the sea floor like a free range fucking colostomy
bag). What in ocean am I saying I am feeling
kinda high and terrified and totally amazing:
fuck poetry, fuck philosophy, fuck biology, fuck
persiflage, no gentle banter this is rock n fucking roll you see   aha   I sea   inside her I am
here, at one with the lifeforce. All feelings of
ethereality are suddenly nullified! I'm a body in
time. I have all these eggs! There were so many it
was a shock when I first released them – like, mil-
lions! Who needs cocaine when you're high off
your own fucking potency! I feel like I was born
to be here. I fucking was! What a sublime joke it
all is. I came here to find lose myself. Lose   hah
a   loose   lost
      last   haha spawn   til I   die oh my

this place is fucking paradise.

I guess that's it for me, folks. If you were hoping to read a story in which life triumphs over

death, the creature doesn't die, illumination is
forthcoming or extinction is averted by an act of
sensitivity or virtue then I must inform

the woman that while I can't predict when her vision will
return, it seems that her unconscious is telling her it's
time to

look at how the light makes gold the edges of things.
Grief, when I allow myself to feel it, makes everything
seem unreal or hyperreal; how painful, how beautiful this can be. The sight in my left eye is returning. I've
held the box containing my sister's ashes. They call them
cremains. They call them larval, glass, silver, juvenile,
mature, semelparous, extinct. My colleagues have been
sending pictures; my eels are all grown up, no longer
transparent but a dark, secret brown. Soon they'll be
ready for the river and then one day the sea. Anything
could happen on their journey. Eels spawn once and then
they die. When you think about it, it's kind of funny.
I could get upset but I have realised that I want to see the
humour in

the best laid plans of eels and men or is it mice
that go awry it rhymes with bye and best intentions curse your questions don't ask me how it
eventuated

I'm not a fucking sage   I'm just
a slick sick fish with a muscular torso gonads
and an anal fin I'm full of BIG SENSATIONS
                                    shooting
spawn in

    new directions

    I'll be slipping off but maybe some of
    my fucking progeny might surface in a
    river, pond or water feature in a neigh-
    bourhood near you. The lucky bitches!
    May they writhe and

    glimmer and

speed through the

    Whatever, you know how it goes.

THE END

*   *   *

EAST: miriamwebster_92@gmail.com

From: submissions@theeasternreview.com.au
          Thank you for your story – we think it's intrigu-
          ing. Edits to come. In response to your question,
          if you're worried about writing from the perspec-
          tive of

SOUTH: *An eel?!* texts my writer friend, crying emoji. Didn't
          we agree that ventriloquising another species seemed

WEST: ridiculous? I know, I say, the next time we have
          coffee. But don't you reckon

NORTH: it's a big relief from the terror of loss to admit that
          it is always, at the same time,

                                              absurd?

A WOMAN, A MAN
AND ANOTHER

ADAM HAS SENSITIVE SKIN. Louise cannot abide it. She thinks Adam is selective about what does and doesn't irritate him. Sometimes it's washing powder, sometimes animals, sometimes gluten. Occasionally, when they are having sex, Adam bails just when things are heating up because the friction, he says, is hurting him. 'Time out,' he says, 'pause. Your skin is touching me too much.' Lately it's the sun. Yes – actual sunshine. She tolerates it, just. She loves him. What else?

For three weeks during the summer break they rent a house in Shoreham. It is a big house belonging to Adam's wealthy second cousin, an environmental consultant who's agreed to rent it to them on the cheap. Before they leave, Adam buys one of those bulk containers of SPF50+ from the discount chemist near their house. It is fluorescent orange and reminds Louise of school and swim club; there is a middle-class pedantry about it that she finds dispiriting.

'Are you actually going to use all that?' she asks him.

'It's good to be prepared,' he retorts.

Adam drives, because Adam is good at driving, which puts Louise in charge of navigation, even though she gets stressed out. They play Hall & Oates, Steely Dan, The Doobie Brothers and Dire Straits – their boomer tunes. She rolls her window down and lets the wind whip hair around her face, resting her hand on Adam's thigh. His skin is greasy from the sunscreen. It is peak season for beachgoers and all along the Mornington Peninsula hordes of tourists glut the shore: the old money set in Portsea, the Greeks with their jacked-up jet skis in Dromana, the big Pacific Islander families round the barbeques at Frankston Beach, the screaming children on the rides at Rye's amusement park. The energy is festive, bordering on deranged, and as they drive Louise feels hopeful, like something is about to shift.

She and Adam have been together since before they were twenty. People say the person you're with in your twenties is not the one you'll be with in your thirties, but Adam thinks that's bullshit. 'They're just jealous,' he says. 'They have no idea.' There was a period where they tried being open and it didn't work, so they went back to being monogamous, acknowledging that the model's flawed. Louise accepts that they have traded the unknown for the familiar and that this involves a little boredom. They share a hypo-allergenic dog named Flossy, an apartment in Thornbury, debt and credit, friends, preferences and ideals. They have two heads for the one electric toothbrush and they know which attributes and flaws they each inherited from their mothers. Louise no longer thinks about other people.

Except—

Except in certain moments, when she sees them riding bikes or eating lunch or drinking out the front of pubs or walking dogs or putting up scaffolding or coming back from the pool or dandling babies and wonders what it would be like if this person were her person, if this baby were her baby, if she had a different life. It's not exactly what she longs for, but still a sense of satisfaction flickers just outside her reach.

When she tries to think about what she wants, everything takes on a horrible significance. She has made a life with Adam, but how much do they really know about each other? What is possible to share and to desire? She thinks about it constantly, desire: how to live with it and how to live it out.

Finally they round a corner and the house emerges from the bush, a large but graceful structure made entirely of steel and glass. The exterior is beautiful, reflecting greenery and clouds as on the surface of a rippling pool. But once inside, Louise begins to feel uneasy. Everything here is clean and soft and neutral, the kind of luxury that has no personality. There are no edges anywhere, no hard lines to mark the border between inside and out. Safer, she thinks, to stand in the middle of the room.

'What's wrong?' Adam asks.

'What?'

'You have a weird look.'

'I do not.'

'You do. Like you hate it.'

'I don't hate it. It's really tasteful.' She walks around a little. 'How rich is your cousin?'

Adam snorts. 'A lot richer than us.'

'Have you been here before?'

'Not since he did the renovations. Look at this,' he says, sliding the door across and standing on the deck. 'It's pretty fucking nice.'

'Yeah, it's nice.'

'Don't sound so enthusiastic.'

She crosses her arms. 'Don't make out like I'm being shitty.'

'You're the one going around criticising everything!' Adam turns his palms upward, like he's appealing to a jury.

'You're making me sound crazy.'

He runs his hands through his hair. 'This is dumb. We've been working really hard to get here. We're on holiday. Why are we arguing?'

He comes and hugs her but she pushes him away.

'What's your problem? As soon as we arrived you started freaking out.'

'I did not freak out,' she says. 'It's because you yelled at me about the navigation. You know I'm shit at Maps.'

'I didn't— I mean, I'm sorry for yelling, alright? I was under pressure, traffic was bad. You were supposed to tell me—'

'To go and get fucked. That's what I should have said.'

'Louise!' he says, holding her shoulders and laughing.

'Stop it. Stop fucking laughing.'

Then before they know it, they are kissing.

'I'm sorry,' he says, breaking the kiss. 'I love you.'

'No, I'm sorry. I don't know why I'm like this.'

'I like how you are. Now,' says Adam. 'Wine?'

They open a bottle of pinot grigio to drink outside. The deck is surrounded by a stylish native garden which is meant to look organic, as though it has spontaneously grown. Whip birds, little wrens and willie wagtails flit amongst the foliage calling pleasantly and past the deck the yard slopes down to meet some paddocks grazed by smooth brown cows, large and placid with their shadows falling on the grass. Further afield, some rows of grapes are growing lush and woody on the hills. Beyond that is the sea.

'You're right,' she says to Adam. 'It's pretty fucking nice.'

They drink and watch the sun go down over the ocean. After a bit of desultory conversation about the weather and the view, their plans for tomorrow and some people that they know, their attention drifts to their phones. Louise can tell from the way Adam's squinting that he is checking the security cameras at work to see if he can catch any of his employees snacking. They're open late during summer, and he has put one of the junior staff in charge.

'Oh my god,' he says suddenly. 'The fucking little—'

'I thought you said you were going to switch off while we're here.'

Adam looks at her like, *don't*. She raises her eyebrows righteously and says, 'Well?'

'Siena's eating the prosciutto.'

She pictures Adam's staff, zombie-like, tearing into joints of meat. It is absurd, but somehow makes her shiver. 'Which one,' she asks, 'the Riserva or the Campanini?'

He zooms in rapidly. 'I can't tell. Fuck. I'm going to have to call them. Can't even leave for *one fucking night*, Louise,' he says, disappearing inside.

Louise leans back against her chair, battling a sinking feeling. Since he and his brother inherited the provedore, Adam has been difficult to reach. It is a business with a long, binding history; his nonno opened the first shop in the sixties after doing time in a labour camp and then on the Snowy Hydro, and the family is focused around it – they celebrate their birthdays there, it's where they do Christmas, it's what they talk about together, it's where they get their food. It seems to cater to the family more than it does customers, and by the time Adam inherited it, the provedore was running at a loss. A butcher by trade, more interested in flesh than figures, he has had to learn quickly and work hard to get it into profit. Louise is happy to be part of it, but there are moments when it feels as though they are oppressed by an entanglement neither of them chose.

'I didn't ask for this,' Adam says.

'So sell it,' says Louise.

'Oh yeah, as if my family would let me.'

Now he comes out carrying his car keys. 'Are you serious?' asks Louise.

'Don't even. I'm just going to go there quickly, sort things out and then I'll come straight back.'

'We just got here. It'll take hours.'

He looks helpless. 'You don't know what it's like.'

Adam does not come back that night, and without him there the house is clinical and creepy; Louise can't move without seeing herself reflected in kilometres of glass. She goes to bed early, feeling annoyed and insecure. In her dreams she is on the verge of a realisation, but the message keeps getting interrupted. There are no curtains in the bedroom and at dawn the day invades the room, pervading it entirely and urging her awake.

She goes out to the deck and looks across the spit of land toward the ocean. The day has come up grey and humid, the sky a slab of cloud rammed flat against the sea. After a while the overcast look of everything begins to feel unglamorous, as if it has been stained in the wash or pissed on by some dogs.

'Where have you been?' she asks, almost hysterical, when Adam finally gets back.

'You're supposed to be taking it easy,' he says. 'We're on holiday. Relax.'

'I am relaxed,' she snaps.

FOR THE NEXT TWO weeks it remains overcast and sprinkles rain from time to time. The windows drag the grey into the house, dulling surfaces and draining things of their vitality. Despite his promise to switch off, Adam is preoccupied with the business and spends much of his time talking on the phone. Even on holiday, their routine takes on a terrible monotony. They sweat it out and snipe at one another, and their sweat is the relentless kind which makes them chafe instead of glow.

'Everything is weird,' Louise sobs one night after too much wine. Adam puts his arms around her, kisses her face and strokes her hair. 'It's okay,' he soothes. 'It will be better in the morning.'

But in the morning it is grey and humid, just like the day before. She and Adam laze around the pool, hungover in a way that seems disproportionate to how much alcohol they actually consumed. A hot northerly skims a film of leaves and grime across the surface.

'I feel awful,' says Louise, slipping off the doughnut floatie.

Adam looks up from his phone. 'You're just hungover.'

Louise pushes off from one side and floats listlessly to the other. The air smells like mushrooms. She inspects her tan, which is coming on slowly, if at all.

'Come on Lou … what's the matter? Are you sick? Are you anxious? Oh my god – are you *pregnant*?'

She looks at him over the top of her sunglasses. 'I wish.'

'Really?'

'No.'

'Okay, well, I'm going inside to reapply. Want some?'

While Adam creams up, Louise looks at her phone. Her mum posts the most out of anyone she knows. She watches reels, signs a petition organised by Teachers 4 Palestine, buys a lipstick and eventually ends up watching a news clip of a massive storm in Queensland which has razed entire towns and dumped the carcasses of cattle on the beach. People are freaking out because a person died. They've named it Helen, which is also the name of her friend who has been living in Berlin. Soon she will return from Europe, and Louise knows that she must see her.

The last time they spoke, Helen said something which Louise had found disturbing. It sounded incongruous at first, but afterward it irked her, and for days Louise had ruminated on her words, failing to understand them. Helen had simply asked if Louise saw herself as a person who goes home when the party's winding down, or someone who stays late, until or past the end.

Louise hadn't known what Helen meant by this.

Even now, she does not know.

Later they go for another swim, this time at the beach. The one they like is mostly empty because of a seaweed problem. Parking the car, they turn themselves out of the aircon and Flossy immediately pelts to where the seaweed is the thickest and most fetid and then rolls in it with wild abandon. Louise wishes she were an animal, doing everything instinctively. Adam strips off his shirt and turns his back to her, handing her the sunscreen. 'Can you do my back?' he asks.

'Again?'

'Yeah, the UV.'

'Is it high, did you check?'

'Eleven.'

'Fine, give it to me.'

'Don't miss any spots,' says Adam. 'I don't want to end up all patchy.'

'Are you going to come in?' she asks once she is done.

'You go. I'll wait for it to sink in.'

She leaves him scrolling on the sand and strokes out far beyond the shore to where the sea is flat and broad, thinking of ways to blow it all up – her life. She could quit her job, go overseas, get pregnant, fall in love with a woman, have an affair, dye her hair, start a new degree, ask Adam for a break. None of it appeals to her; the solutions are boring because her crisis is routine.

Flipping on her back she thinks again of Helen. Once, on holiday with a group of friends, they had a threesome with a drummer. It was the only time Louise had been unfaithful – she and Adam had been dating for about a year. It was not a bad experience but not a good one either; she and Helen were too close as friends to be intimate as lovers, and the entire thing felt staged.

Helen was thin and elegant and incisive, like a sharp, expensive knife. Louise was tall and soft and talkative, though at times she could be shy. At first they played up their differences, how they complemented one another, which drove the drummer wild. But then at some point Helen decided she was over it and left the room, taking all the glamour with her. Louise had felt jilted, like a lover spurned. There didn't seem any point in going on without her, though a sense of obligation made her stay and finish the job.

Afterward, Helen asked if it had changed Louise's feelings about Adam. 'Are you going to break up?'

'No,' Louise had said. If anything, it was clear that she loved Adam and preferred to be in a relationship. The failed threesome was a minor aberration. But maybe that's what Helen meant, she thinks now, when she asked Louise if she was someone who would stay until the end.

That night, she and Adam watch a movie where a group of storm chasers have a series of dangerous, passionate encounters with tornadoes and each other. Its cheap erotic thrill is stupid and it makes them horny so they start to mess around. While she is giving him head, his breath catches in his throat. It is only when he gargles slightly that she realises he's asleep. 'Adam,' she says sharply. 'Adam. Are you *sleeping?*'

'Huh? No. What?'

'You were snoring! Is it that fucking boring? How do you fall asleep with your cock in my mouth?'

'Mmn,' he mumbles, sinking back against the couch. He looks exactly like a sated baby disengaging from the nipple, his mouth open slightly, the sweet curve of his nose. There is a greediness about him that she finds unnerving, a sense of entitlement. He has flung his arm against the pillow. She wants to hurt him. She can't hate him. Gently, she puts his cock back in his pants. 'Love you,' he says sleepily.

It prompts in her a shiver of abjection. Not disgust, exactly. There is love and fear in it, too.

Restless, she gets up from the couch and roams the house, opening cupboards and turning on taps, but it's the kind of place which has no secrets. She laments the lack of narrow passages and shadowed corners, places where it would be possible to begin.

What does she mean, begin?

She means to start *the work*: the delicate task of beguiling all these disparate aspects of herself into a whole.

AT THE BEGINNING OF the last week of their holiday, Adam goes back to Melbourne for a day to help out in the shop. Louise says nothing, trying hard to be magnanimous. 'I'll bring us back some treats,' he promises.

'You fucking better,' says Louise.

The next day Adam returns with a bunch of flowers, prosecco and a bottle of Montenegro to make spritzes, vegetables, meat, fish, bread, charcuterie and several different types of cheese. Louise prepares lunch, setting herself the task of celebrating each ingredient, as Adam's nonno used to say. They take a tablecloth, wine, cutlery and plates and carry it all down the back, where they spread out on the grass to eat. The air is heavy and it finally looks like it might rain. Once they have eaten, Louise lies back against the grass. She is full and suddenly quite emotional. She reaches for Adam's hand. He squeezes hers, as if to say, 'I understand.' Everything is beautiful. Everything feels pregnant with meaning.

'Is that your phone?' he asks. Louise looks around and finds that it has slipped under the tablecloth they've been using as a picnic rug. It is Helen. She doesn't answer.

'Who is it?'

'Helen.'

'Fucking hell. What does she want?'

'I don't know.'

'Are you going to answer it?'

'No.'

'Good.'

'Adam, you're being an arsehole.' She bends down and starts stacking their dishes, intending to carry them inside. Adam looks hurt, but also slightly righteous. She feels bad. He loves her. He is trying to make her happy.

'I love you,' he says on cue.

How to reassure him?

'I have to call her back,' she says, marching up the sloping yard to make the call inside.

She recalls what Helen said the first time she met Adam. 'He's nice Louise, but is he really on your *level*? What does he do again?'

'He's a butcher,' she'd replied.

Helen had wrinkled her nose. 'His hands must always smell of meat.'

'Not really.' She didn't say, *we fuck like we mean it and eat every part of the beast.*

Trying Helen's WhatsApp, she thinks: Adam is gorgeous. Adam is kind and perceptive and his hands do not always smell of meat. Sometimes they smell of herbs. Sometimes they smell of Turkish delight. Sometimes they smell of Parmigiano Reggiano and sometimes soap, especially when he gets home from the shop. Lately, Adam's hands smell of sunscreen. Helen cannot know this, because Helen doesn't care. She thinks Adam is parochial, and he thinks Helen's an elitist. Both are true to some degree. Adam has blind faith in work and family and an aspirational model for creating wealth. Helen's parents are left-wing intellectuals, which makes her wonderful and generous, and the most vicious kind of snob. Their mutual contempt is something Louise has not been able to reconcile.

Finally, Helen answers.

'My flight gets in on Friday,' she declares. 'And I was thinking I would come and stay.'

FIRST THING ON FRIDAY morning, before it is even light, Flossy leaps from the bed, raises her hackles and emits a low, unusual growl. When Louise lets her outside she runs into the yard, fixes on something in the near distance and begins to bark hysterically. It is somehow spooky. Louise calls her inside.

There is a sachet of smoked salmon in the fridge that needs to be eaten before it goes off. In the kitchen, she turns on lights and makes coffee, wondering what to do with it. She takes it out and removes the packaging. The flesh triggers an association with Helen, perhaps a dream she's had but can't particularly recall.

Adam walks in looking sleepy. 'What time is it?'

'Early,' says Louise.

'Why are we up?'

She sips her coffee and says instead, 'Helen's back today.'

Adam puts his hands on the bench. 'And?'

'She was thinking of heading down here for the weekend,' she says.

'When, exactly?'

'This afternoon.'

'Seriously?' Adam exhales loudly.

'Can you stop breathing so aggressively and like, say what you want to say?'

'Okay Louise, you want to hear what I have to say? Helen is a fucking user. She's in it for the free holiday. She finds out we're staying in this amazing house, gets back and sniffs us out. And you're just going to let her do it, like always.'

'Fuck off Adam,' says Louise. 'She wants to see me.' But she is disturbed by the way he said she *sniffed them out*.

Adam is flushed with excitement. 'She's so transparent, but she acts like she's this great unsolvable mystery. It's unbearable.'

Disquieted, Louise plates up the salmon. She has read that no one knows why salmon jump; there are various hypotheses but essentially their behaviour is inexplicable. Now she imagines the fillets leaping off the bench, brought back by some odd galvanism. Softly, as though to the fish she says, 'I still find her mysterious.'

Adam watches her intently. 'You've already said yes, haven't you?'

'It's only a couple of nights.'

'Fucking hell,' he says quietly, taking his breakfast things and stalking from the room. She hears the television come on and then the rousing melody which accompanies a special broadcast. There is the phrase, *unusually severe*. She follows Adam into the loungeroom and sits next to him on the couch.

'Check this out,' he says, their argument over Helen momentarily forgotten. 'There's going to be a massive storm.'

The audio is slightly out of sync, so there's a delay each time the newsreader speaks.

We interrupt this morning's normal programming to bring you news of a severe weather event Adam raises the volume *set to make landfall later this afternoon. Meteorologists have identified a low—* he changes channels *pressure system which is set to interact with exceptionally high ocean temperatures, causing catastrophic storm conditions, extremely dangerous, peaking at Category* five minutes later, all the news channels are reporting the same thing, how *populations have been put on high alert, as well as SES teams across* the sky outside begins to bruise and 'Fucking hell,' says Adam again, as the dog pins back her ears and hides behind them on the *low-lying areas of the Peninsula will need to be evacuated* says the newsreader, slight delay, as *State Government officials meet this morning to discuss which measures will be taken* there is already footage of congestion on the roads.

They open the weather app but it's glitching and won't load.

Ten minutes later, they see on the news that the weather app has crashed.

While the experts try to bring it back online, Louise and Adam check their socials, where conspiracies have already started circulating. Adam refreshes the feed, his amusement giving way to anger. 'Can you believe these people?' he asks.

'Madness,' says Louise. But in some way she does understand it. The hysteria. The impulse to see portents, the desire to speculate. Like the conspiracists she finds herself hoping that the storm contains a message, as if she is calling on it to produce a kind of knowledge.

'I wonder if we should do anything to prepare?' she asks.

'We've got until four.'

'That's when Helen's meant to be arriving.'

Adam is almost smirking. 'Oh, really? I guess she'll have to come another time.'

Feeling intrepid, they walk down to the beach. The atmosphere has changed, a frisson hums around them and their hair lifts in the static. Flossy sniffs the air, runs and sniffs again. The morning comes up palely, a sunrise not of colour but of shade. Suddenly, Louise feels her excitement plummet; it is the same as all the other days – grey. She walks down to the shoreline, where waves lay their promise to waste: the sand, the sea, the swimmers are grey, the bloodless sky, the manky froth and shat-upon rocks, the gulls and cranes and broken shells, the books on towels – fifty shades of summer reading. Terrible tourists have left plastic and aluminium behind, wrappers that the sea has tumbled to a dullish shade, and heat has bleached the seaweed, stripping picnic tables of their stain. Adam's sunscreen catches fluff like office carpet. Today was supposed to mean something. It is crushing to think that it is simply, grey.

She swims out past the waves as usual and flips onto her back. The ocean ripples slightly, as if a shiver courses underneath. On the beach, in the distance, Adam is looking at his phone. She can tell he's agitated by the way he jigs his leg. Flossy lingers by his side, panting worriedly. Louise waves. Suddenly he rises and, as if compelled by unknown forces, walks straight into the sea.

She finds herself moving. Something thrills her, drawing her to Adam. Reaching the shallows, she stands and walks toward him. The dog is barking madly. The tide has drawn itself a long way out. Adam leaps forward, smiling in an odd way, not quite laughing. He scoops Louise into his arms.

For a moment they hold each other's gaze and Adam's body is so warm and dry against her own, which is cool and slippery from her swim. A quick charge bristles between them, an erotic force which speaks to something more than sex. Louise believes that in this moment she and Adam feel they're on the threshold of an experience. *This is it*, she thinks. *This will change the way we live.*

Then there is a sudden slap of thunder, and he drops Louise into the sea.

'We'd better go,' he says.

She agrees.

BACK AT THE HOUSE, Adam goes into action mode. He fills the bathtub and the wheelie bins with water, rummages in the shed for torches and candles and goes through the cupboard for canned food. They keep track of the storm, reading stats and watching footage shot from space, anxiously discussing changes to its fearsome eye and tentacles of swirling, lethal cloud. The weatherman is young and gay and as the storm predictions worsen he becomes excited, like he's about to scream or dance around the newsroom. By midday, the storm has been upgraded. The weatherman looks like he's on drugs and has been partying for several days: his hair is tousled and his shirt has come unbuttoned. He makes intense eye contact with the camera as he predicts a superstorm. 'That's right Michelle,' he says, turning back to his colleagues. 'The biggest storm this state has ever seen.'

The Premier declares a state of emergency, evacuates low-lying regions and urges those at higher elevation to prepare. Now there is footage of sandbagging in the beachside suburbs. Whole swathes of the city have been pre-emptively taken off the grid.

News travels quickly. Adam's cousin emails with instructions for storm proofing the house. They find a ladder and start working on the gutters. The humidity reaches ninety-five per cent. Beneath the sweat Louise can feel excitement mounting once again. From the roof she can see all the way to where the land is licked at by the ocean; everything feels kind of sexual, the call of the unknown.

Helen texts to say she's on the train.

'I can't believe it,' says Adam. 'Is she out of her fucking mind?'

Louise has no choice but to collect her from the station. Driving toward Frankston, a fatalistic part of her imagines that the storm will hit while she is on the road, the car felled by a tree. She sees the wheels spinning, the windscreen smashed, her body crumpled on a scary angle, blood. Imagines Adam's face the moment he gets the call.

Arriving early, she goes to the plaza for supplies. The shelves are empty, reminding her of lockdowns they endured in the pandemic. People are pushing each other out of the way. Her mouth fills briefly with the tang of panic as she scans the aisles with a feeling for the end of days. She walks out carrying whatever they had left – a box of frozen spinach, some lavosh crackers, a small round tin of caviar.

Parked outside the station, she rolls the window down and looks for Helen. The sky is jaundiced with a sickly yellow hue and everything looks backlit, giving objects in the foreground haloes like those tiny, coloured cards her grandma used to show her with the pictures of the saints. Helen is already waiting, dressed in a white linen shift. Despite the chaos all around her, she looks beautifully composed.

She remembers the first time she visited Helen's family home, being struck not by the size or beauty of the house, or the parents' excellent taste in everything, but by the bookshelves lining all the walls. In her own house growing up there had been books about pruning, music, food;

they contained instructions. But Helen's family home was crammed with books about *ideas*. Louise was so impressed that she was almost frightened. She desperately wanted to be intimate with Helen and to live the way she lived.

Finally Helen sees her, waves and waits to cross the road. Despite her flaws, Louise loves her. She admires her self-assurance. Helen knows exactly where she's going. In contrast, Louise is thrashing around blindly, striving to answer a question.

But she doesn't know what question she is asking.

THE ROADS ARE DEAD as they drive back to Shoreham. For some reason, neither of them mention the storm. Instead they hold hands across the console, Louise listening as Helen describes her time abroad.

As Helen speaks, a tremendous wind rolls in. It buffets the car and starts to sweep the sky of clouds. Louise feels panicky, as though she has been tricked. Just as quickly as it came, the wind dies down and leaves the sky a spanking shade of blue.

They drive through light and dappled shade and it gets hot and dreamy in the car. Helen's speech begins to lull Louise into a kind of torpor. She finds it difficult to focus on the road. It's a nice feeling, seductive. They fall into a treacly silence until Helen says, from out of nowhere, 'Do you think that you and Adam fit together? What about me and Adam. Do you think we'd fit, him and me?'

'Why would you—'

'I met someone in Berlin,' she says. 'We ended up living together. He was an artist, quite successful, with this spacious apartment in the city. When I first started sleeping there I found the entire place so neat and impersonal it seemed like a pretence, as if he'd borrowed it from a friend and was faking living there because he wanted to impress me. There weren't any toiletries in the bathroom – no razors, cologne, no creams or packets of pills. It was bizarre. I got really suspicious and began to think he must have a secret partner or a family somewhere else, where he really lived, even though he claimed that he was free.

'I started looking in cupboards and under the beds when he was out of the house. It felt duplicitous, but I had this crazed desire to discover evidence he was lying. You know I've never been really jealous of anyone, and mostly my relationships have been open. But I became completely paranoid. Possessive. And I never found anything, no matter where I looked.'

Here she pauses, still clasping Louise's hand. Her grip is almost desperate and Louise feels superior for the first time ever. It is an odd sensation. She moves her hand away.

'Maybe that feeling arose from being away from home,' Louise ventures. 'You needed this man, this domestic arrangement, to provide the security you were missing.'

'Maybe. But the weirdest thing was, I was right. He *did* have a secret family, two kids with a previous partner. He just mentioned them one morning as if they'd been a fact of our relationship from the beginning, and then a couple of days later they came to live with us at the apartment.'

Helen turns now and Louise can feel her staring at the side of her own face, though she keeps her eyes glued to the road. She has a strong sense of not wanting to hear the rest of the story; at the same time she is curious to learn how it played out, and what made Helen stay.

'How old were his children?'

'Five and eight, two girls. They're beautiful kids. I just...'

Louise supposes Helen is about to say she couldn't accept her partner's children, no matter how great they were, because of the betrayal. But then she says, quite unexpectedly, 'We became extremely close. I want to say the four of us fell in love. You know me, Lou – I'm not maternal. I didn't expect to feel so passionate about this family life I'd never wanted, but as soon as I met them it was like something fell into place. I felt as though we'd always been together and I'd been missing them after a long absence, as if they'd been away at school camp. It sounds stupid, but I felt as though the children had come home. Like their home was with me, like we fit together. But then—'

Her revelation halts with crunching gravel as Louise turns up the drive. The splendid house looms from the bush like a sculpture or museum, and for a second Helen is distracted, taking it all in. Louise recalls how Adam said that Helen sniffed them out. She feels a little nauseous. Helen winds the window down and inhales in a big, exaggerated way.

'Smell that air,' she murmurs, feigning a kind of bliss.

Louise inhales too. The air smells good; the wind has made things clean.

Hearing the car, Adam emerges from the house. His face is grim and unsmiling.

What happened next, Louise wants to ask. *And how did you leave? And what is the difference between us or are we the same, you and me?*

But Helen is already out of the car, pretending to be happy to see Adam, and the time for candour is gone.

AS HE LEADS THEM to the room where Helen will be staying, Adam is cordial and even pleasant. Louise walks behind the pair and wonders what the hell they're up to, herself included. The clean white walls and carpets seem suddenly fake, as though the three of them are play acting on the set of a television show, or the large characterless apartment in Berlin that Helen just described. In the bedroom, Helen deposits her bag and then they all go to the kitchen. Everyone is smiling. It's incredibly bizarre.

On the deck they sit around a table where the shady gums protect them from the heat. Louise opens the lavosh crackers and the caviar she bought at the plaza. It's not quite right as far as platters go, but it will have to do. She smells the sea. When she takes a sip of wine and licks her lips, they taste of minerals and salt.

'Whoa,' exclaims Helen. 'Caviar. I would eat some, but I've been a practicing vegan for about a year.'

Adam snorts, and Louise can tell he's taken umbrage at the phrase *practicing vegan*. 'I might have been tempted,' Helen adds, 'if you'd bought my favourite.'

Louise cannot remember Helen's favourite. 'It was fairly apocalyptic at the shops,' she says instead.

'I can imagine! I thought my flight would be delayed. What happened to the storm?'

'It's weird,' says Adam. 'All morning we thought it was coming. We even did all the preparations. But now the weather is completely fine – better than it's been the whole time we've been here.'

'I can't help feeling cheated,' Helen says. 'There are things I need clarified. You know what I mean?'

'Not really,' says Adam.

Yes, thinks Louise.

Helen leans forward and puts her elbows on the table. 'Don't you think there's something absolutely momentous about a storm? It's the sort of thing that inspires people to act.'

Adam snorts again. 'If you mean fighting over toilet rolls, then sure.'

Helen looks at Adam and dismisses him, like he's a rock or stick she picked up off the ground, considered for a moment and then failed to apprehend.

'I wanted it,' Louise says ardently, startling herself. 'I wanted to experience the storm. Do you ever feel like you are waiting...'

'Yes,' says Helen simply. She turns to Adam. 'Maybe it's something men like you can't understand.'

'What do you mean, *like me?*'

Helen ignores him. 'I missed you, Lou.'

'I'm sure you say that to all your fans.'

'Shut up Adam,' says Louise.

'You think I'm being facetious,' says Helen, 'but I mean it. There were things I loved about Berlin ...'

Louise thinks she will resume her story from the car, but Helen shakes herself and smiles. 'There were things I loved about it, but I didn't have many friends. I was rarely alone, but even so, I think I was often lonely.'

There is a pause. Standing behind her, Helen begins to stroke Louise's arms and shoulders, running her hands over the skin. It is so nice to be touched. Adam watches this display with annoyance, grabbing the sunscreen he has brought outside and placed before them on the table. He squirts a generous amount into his palm and rubs his own arms furiously, applying far more than he needs.

'Is that why you came back?' Adam asks, rising quickly from the table.

Helen looks away, toward the rows of vines. 'No,' she says quietly. 'No, it's not.'

Unsatisfied, Adam goes inside to find another bottle. While he is gone, Louise turns to Helen. 'So you left them?' she asks softly.

'I left them,' Helen replies.

'But you loved them,' Louise says.

'I did. But living with them permanently was not part of my plan.'

'You couldn't have changed it?'

'You've known me for a long time, Lou. Once I've decided on a course, I never change my mind.'

Louise thinks of the superstorm and how it should be making landfall now. 'Not even if it would have made you happy?' she asks.

'Are you happy?'

'I'm not unhappy,' Louise replies. 'I know better than to expect happiness from life.'

Helen's eyes flash with a certain cruelty, which instantly disappears. 'Sooner or later, Louise, you're going to have to act.'

THEY KEEP DRINKING, AND because there is nothing else to eat they soon get very drunk. Night falls so gradually they hardly register the change, until suddenly it's dark and stars are numerous in the sky. Helen disappears and comes out wearing a gorgeous slip dress in a silky green material. It clings like water to her body, showing off her pointy nipples and the delicate ridges of her hips.

'Thought I'd slip into something more comfortable,' she says, mock seductively, although Louise glances at Adam and can tell by the look on his face that some part of the seduction is real.

Strangely, she does not feel envious or upset. Above them, the sky has clouded over. The clouds are low and round, pregnant with moisture. The humidity rackets up.

A rough wind stirs the dust and leaves and then dies out. Once more, the air is still.

A fine sweat shimmers on Louise's forehead; absently she wipes it off. The sense of being actors on a set returns and everything moves slowly. The camera pans the deck. We see Helen's laughing mouth, Adam raising his glass, Adam looking at Louise, Helen looking at Louise, Adam looking at Helen, Louise wiping her brow. Then it stops and time resumes its normal pace.

There is music playing in the house. Adam goes inside to turn it up and when he comes outside again, Helen is dancing in that lustrous green dress, pulling Louise from her seat and spinning her around, pressing her body against Louise's like they did to impress that drummer, or how they used to tease the private school boys at their university soirees. As they dance, Louise tilts her chin up to the sky, closing her eyes for just a moment, feeling Helen's slippery dress against her body and the sensation of being spun very fast and close to the earth, like being on the whizzy dizz at the park when she was smaller. When she opens her eyes again it's late and one thing has led to another. The house is dark and Helen has invited herself – or they've invited her – into their bed.

It is different to last time. Distance and the years have opened up a space between Louise and Helen and it feels like a first encounter. But the roles have been reversed; now it is Louise who thinks of leaving, glancing at the door to the bedroom which would take her down the hall and into quiet. *Is she the kind of person who leaves when the party's winding down, or someone who stays late, until or past the end?*

She finds herself standing alone at the foot of the bed. Sooner or later ...

'Wait,' says Adam, lightly panting. 'Louise.'

Adam reaches for her with his eyes, trying to draw her back into their tryst. His desire is oppressive and she has a shocking thought: right now, all she wants to do is give it all away. Their life of luxury, their love, this strange and spacious house. And she realises she is angry with the failure of the storm.

Adam says her name again, 'Louise.'

'Helen,' she says.

'No,' says Adam. 'Louise.'

'Louise,' says Helen.

'Helen,' says Louise.

'It's okay ... I know. Come here ...' Helen reaches for her arm. The pressure of her hand is gentle, but so insistent that finally it is all Louise can do to play her part.

Later, she has no idea what time, she wakes with a strange sense of anticipation. On one side of her is Adam, sleeping greedily. On the other, Helen lies so quietly it's like she hardly even breathes. Flossy has curled up on the floor at their feet, put out at having been displaced, and the rough wind is back, throwing sticks and sand against the glass. Louise lies still and listens. She thinks she knows the nature of her question: a dynamic has shifted, something's been distilled.

Gently, she rouses her sleeping friend. Helen stirs and turns to face her, although her eyes remain closed.

'Helen … when you said I forgot to get your favourite. What did you mean?'

'My favourite …'

'The one you mentioned earlier, when I served the caviar. Your favourite. I can't remember.'

'Oh …' Helen murmurs sleepily. 'Smoked salmon. I don't eat it anymore, since I'm a—'

'Practicing vegan, yeah, but—'

'I love it all the same,' she sighs. 'I thought you knew that, but maybe we're not as close as we used to be.'

She lets her words hang between them and Louise can't tell whether it is out of sleepiness, malice, sincerity or need. Adam stirs, demanding more of the blanket, and suddenly she leaps from the bed, sick of lying there between them.

'Where are you going?' Helen murmurs. 'Come back—'

But her command is interrupted by the first hard slap of rain. Louise braces herself, for at this very moment, right above the house and only now that she has ceased to miss it, the storm has gathered itself and finally, resoundingly, arrives.

PEDUNCLE SLAP

AUGUST ARRIVED ON THE wind, a chill southerly blowing off Bass Strait. I heard the humpbacks were migrating and suddenly felt inspired to take the children on a whale watching tour.

Our hope for the tour was to see a peduncle slap. This was the part, so my eldest daughter told me, when the whale stuck its tail out of the water and slapped it down on the surface with a big, resounding thwack. My daughter was almost five years old and clever, which is not to say she's prodigious, just that she pays acute attention to language. She got 'peduncle' from a nature documentary and remembered it, this word I'd never heard.

Behaviouralists wonder whether peduncle slapping constitutes an act of aggression or one of jouissance – if whales can be said to possess psychic tonalities such as these.

I searched *peduncle slapping* on the internet and found conflicting theories: some called it a playful ritual and others called it a warning. I wondered what humpbacks meant by this magnificent show of force and what emotions spurred it on. If we saw a humpback on the tour, would it slap its tail for us? Would it seem joyous or intimidating? Did we have the right to watch it?

These questions preoccupied me as I pulled up outside my mother-in-law's house in the bristling dark of a Thursday morning. The forecast told me that the day would be windy but fine, although it currently seemed cloudy. The weather bureau was always getting it wrong. I'd heard they had a toxic culture of bullying and climate denial, which did not surprise me. You couldn't work with weather and feel generous all the time. I looked at the sky through my windscreen; there were hardly any stars.

I thought my mother-in-law must be lonely. I was lonely too, but in a different way, because Alex was always travelling for work, leaving me alone with the children. My kids were cool, but I missed adult conversation. I felt like I was always waiting for Al to come home, for the children to grow up, for my favourite TV show to air, for my life to come back into focus. I supposed that many women felt this way. My mother-in-law probably experienced these feelings herself, when Alex was a boy.

Now she was constantly inviting herself over and had insisted on coming with us on the whale watching tour. I had wanted to take the kids myself; I felt like it was an important moment for the three of us to share and rehearsed what I would say to them about the value of respecting nature. Alex and I wanted our children to grow up with a deep connection to the natural world. We had chosen to have them in an era of catastrophe and species loss; the least we could do was nurture this connection so they might feel inspired to protect it in their turn.

My mother-in-law was taking ages to leave her house. I texted her to say we were waiting outside and leaned back against the seat to wait, impatience making me tap my hand against the steering wheel.

'Why are you tapping Mummy?' asked my eldest daughter.

I told her I was tapping along to a song in my head.

'What song?' she asked.

The younger one, whose habit lately was to imitate her sister, said, 'What song Mummy? What song?'

We sang a song from one of their shows and I felt a little tired.

Just then, my mother-in-law opened the passenger door. 'What's this song?' she asked the girls cheerily. They started teaching her how it went and I felt relieved that there was someone else to entertain them. Perhaps it was a good thing she was coming, after all.

As I drove, I thought about our relationship. I struggled to understand the ambivalence I felt toward her. It was not that I didn't like her, but that I couldn't help playing hostage to her sudden wills and idiosyncrasies. After she visited my house, I would often find her long white hairs on my furniture and shiver. They were never brittle, as I'd imagined, but very, very strong, and I always equated this with the force of my mother-in-law's personality. She never changed her behaviour to suit other people, a trait which made me furious, even though seeing it in someone else might have prompted me to say that it was something I admired.

When we were together, she liked to tell me stories. Alex is an only child so there have never been other people to give an account of his early years. At the beginning of our relationship I loved hearing these stories, how fondly she would speak about this or that event in Al's childhood, but when I asked him about it later, he would often say that wasn't how it happened. The reality was different – not as romantic as his mother had described.

Lately, I had even noticed her taking liberties in recounting things we'd done together, which really started to disturb me. I thought that left unchecked I could end up this way too, for I worried that I had a similar tendency to rearrange things in my memory, remembering feelings as facts, becoming nostalgic for people and places which were never that good to begin with.

The heating was turned up and my mother-in-law asked if she could turn it down. 'Yeah, if you want,' I said, 'or you could take your parka off.'

She was wearing this wildly outdated ski jacket I knew had seen her through two winters in Germany, where she'd met my husband's father; she had told me this story a hundred times before. Al maintained his father was an arsehole, but I knew it was more complex than that. Still, my mother-in-law's voice got misty as she told it and I felt annoyed again and slightly panicked trying to decode the slippery blend of fact and fiction in her tale.

My mother-in-law navigated while I got us onto the freeway. She was a good navigator actually, giving me lots of time to prepare for all the turns. I liked being together with her in this way, doing something practical. It would take about two hours to drive to Phillip Island, but once we were on the freeway the route was nice and straightforward.

My daughters were misbehaving and I asked her to hand each of them a device. The car pinged with the carnival sounds of games and I said to turn it down so I could better hear my mother-in-law's directions. A funereal morning spread itself across the horizon and I felt dispirited. All I could do was tell myself that everything would be okay as soon as we saw a whale. I tried to imagine how I would feel, seeing a humpback slap its tail against the heaving ocean. It felt good. I told my mother-in-law I was certain that seeing a peduncle slap would restore us to a sense of the world's majesty, and she agreed.

Closer to the coast, the wind was strong. Alex texted me to ask if we had seen a whale yet, and my mother-in-law read it out.

'Tell him we're not there yet, it was an early start and everyone is tired, but we're all feeling excited to see a peduncle slap,' I dictated as my mother-in-law replied on my behalf.

'I'm just going to add, *wish you were here*. What do you think?'

'I think that's good,' I said. 'Maybe say something about the weather too, how it's windy and looking a bit grey.'

'The more detail, the better, I think.'

'Actually, wait, delete that. Al hates it when I give too much detail. He says it makes him feel obliged to reply in kind, but that he's just at work so there is nothing interesting to say.'

'Yes, he's funny like that,' said his mother. 'Always trying to narrow things down, to make them streamlined. I suppose it's no coincidence that he works as a consultant, overhauling all those businesses, improving their systems. But I sometimes think … all that stripping – what a waste!'

What she said was completely true. Alex had an aversion to complexity. It drove me crazy. But he must have learned to do this somewhere, at some point. He must have learned that in order to understand things, he needed to whittle them down.

'He does do that, doesn't he?' I remarked. 'It makes me so annoyed.'

The conversation turned to other things that annoyed us. My mother-in-law told inane stories about people from her past who had wronged her in minute ways for things which should have been forgotten, though she cherished these resentments and seemed to draw from them great funds of agitation and delight. She didn't want to let up so I employed a method I'd developed when I was a member of the student union, being lectured by opinionated social-ists, of letting their words wash over me, listening to their cadence without trying to grasp their meaning, using my knowledge of their phrasing and intonation to insert occa-sional sounds – *hmmm, aha, mnn* – which made it seem like I was listening.

Now, if I zoned out successfully, my mother-in-law's droning would have produced a hypnotic feeling, not unlike ASMR. But today I had to concentrate because of the gale. I could not seem to hit the perfect point at which I was disengaged though responsive enough to have that pleasant feeling.

ON THE ROAD TO Rhyll we passed SES teams in high-vis, chainsawing fallen timber into rounds. My daughters thought they looked like giant wheels of cheese and my mother-in-law reminded us that she was lactose intolerant, which made me want to hurt her in some tiny, precise way. The weather was increasingly wild and I wondered if we would get a refund should the tour today be cancelled. Al hated spending money on frivolous things and thought that whale watching should wait for a time when we were better off. I told him that with the oceans getting warmer, the whales might not visit at such a time. It sounded overly dramatic.

Dark clouds massed over the horizon as we queued for the boat, a large white catamaran called the *Suellen*. My children seemed to like it; *Soooo-wellen,* they chanted, rounding their lips. The wind performed its frigid ministry and my mother-in-law said it made her feel enlivened, like something inconceivable was about to occur. In her life, windy days brought unexpected tidings, like a gift in the mail or news of an old flame.

She did not ask me for a wind story of my own, so I didn't say that I grew up in the central deserts, where the air is always still. When I first moved to the city – before I met her son – I felt constantly skittish, like a frightened mare. People in the street, I am sure, saw too much white in my eyes. I stopped using umbrellas because the wind always turned them inside out, exposing their spokes as if they had been flayed.

My mother-in-law insisted we sit at the front of the boat where I knew it would be freezing. When I said so, she said I should have worn a warmer jacket, like the German one she was wearing, which had seen her through several winters on the Continent around the time she met Al's dad and so on. She did the zipper up to her chin and made a little wiggling motion which indicated she was toasty. We sat on a low bench coated white with paint and bird shit, watching the pier recede until the island was a distant thought behind us. The boat sluiced through the surf and between spray and rain we were getting quite wet. I held onto my youngest daughter and looked over the sea, which was powerful and grey.

I suddenly felt ambivalent about seeing a whale. The more I thought about it, the more I realised they confronted me. During my research for the whale watching tour I had come across a story on the internet about the Loneliest Whale, also known as 52 Blue, a whale of unknown species who sang at a higher frequency than any other whale. She was believed to be female, although no one had ever seen her in the flesh, only recorded her song via hydrophone, a song which was totally incommunicable to others of her kind. On the Wikipedia page, I clicked on a sound bite and listened. It struck me as impossibly sad.

I began to think about how hard it was to make other people understand you. This was something I tried to do with Al. I was always explaining myself, and Al tried his best to get it. But somehow, we failed to meet each other halfway. With him gone for work so often I felt like we were missing out on each other's lives. I sent him pictures of the children, accompanied by lengthy texts about our days, and he usually replied with 'Sounds fun' or 'Wow, that looks nice.' This didn't feel like enough.

Just then, the boat crested a massive wave and startled us, causing my mother-in-law to clutch my hand in fear. Weirdly moved, I put my arm around her, squeezing her puffy shoulder.

There passed a period of wind, rain and sea in which nothing unusual happened save for the momentous cresting of the *Suellen*. The boat arrived at a seal colony strangely devoid of seals, as if they had agreed by popular vote to disappear. All we smelled was a thick mammalian stench that seemed to linger in the foamy wake.

I could no longer deny that the weather was inclement. I frantically refreshed the app, hoping it would change. My children asked us when we would see a whale and we told them to be patient. The waves got bigger. I did not feel entirely safe.

At one point we thought we saw a white tail, which from a distance really did look like a humpback's famous peduncle slap. We could almost hear the *thwack*, but when the boat edged closer, we saw we'd been deceived: it was just another foam-capped wave.

THE *SUELLEN* SHUDDERED AND I realised we had forgotten to take our ginger tablets; I could picture them now, left behind on the kitchen bench. My mother-in-law complained that she was seasick, stumbling to the railings and dry retching, and my daughters and I felt concerned. An announcement requested all patrons come inside. The tour would be turning back because of the weather, and regrettably, due to running costs, the operating company could not issue any refunds.

In the vast cabin it was stiflingly hot and smelled like vomit. My mother-in-law said she was glad to be turning back; being out here was *hell*. I felt increasingly distressed and guilty for making us all come on this disastrous tour. I realised that I wanted my mother-in-law to act the parent – after all, she was the most senior person here – by reassuring me and the children that it was okay, we would soon be back on shore, it didn't matter if we didn't see a whale, whatever. Instead, she said I looked stricken.

'You look like you're on the absolute *verge*,' she said dramatically. 'How do I look? I don't feel well. I'm too hot! Quick, give me one of those bags.'

I handed her a seasickness bag and she stuck her face into it and heaved. Watching her vomit made me anxious; I was not feeling seasick but I feared the children would see or smell it and start vomiting too. I rushed around, gathering more bags. When I returned to our seats my mother-in-law was clutching the neck of her parka: 'I'm too hot, I'm too hot, I'm burning up,' she kept saying. I told her to unzip it – better yet to take it off – but she either failed to hear me or pretended not to.

I was glad I wasn't sick, though I did feel on the verge of panic, as my mother-in-law had said. She looked really terrible, she was sweating and her face had turned an ashy grey. She tried to clutch my hand again but I was busy with the children, helping them take off their coats, making sure they had water, attentive just in case they were about to spew. I sensed her hand fall and then her shoulders droop unhappily, but I didn't have the capacity then to do anything about it.

My children asked again if we would see any whales, and I said, probably not. There was some commotion by the toilets and we noticed a gathering of people and staff near to the adjacent stairs. They were crowded around someone or something on the floor. I tried to see what they were looking at but there were too many people in the way. 'What's happening?' my mother-in-law was saying, notes of panic in her voice.

'I don't know,' I said, 'I'm trying to see but I can't tell.'

'What, what is it Grandma?' said my children, catching onto our hysteria. I sensed we'd reached a tipping point and tried to calm us down.

'It's okay, don't worry about it,' I said, as much to them as to myself. 'Someone must have spilled something on the floor.'

'Vomit, most likely,' ventured my mother-in-law, and for a blissful second, we laughed.

When the boat docked back at the pier, we gathered ourselves as best we could and shuffled off. On the pier an ambulance was parked. A group of paramedics rushed past with a trolley.

'What's happening?' asked my mother-in-law again, but the paramedics did not answer.

'Someone was ill,' said a fellow passenger walking beside us on the pier. 'An older woman, I think. She got so seasick she went into hypovolemic shock and then, well … I saw them put her in a bag.'

'They put her in a *bag*?' asked my eldest daughter, eyes wide.

'To keep her warm,' said my mother-in-law quickly. We shared a glance. We did not wish to tell the children somebody had died.

THE CHILDREN WERE SILENT as we walked through the car park. I asked my mother-in-law if she was feeling any better and she said she felt alright. 'I can't believe I said ... God, I'm so dramatic. To think that a woman actually—' she leaned into me and whispered, '*died*.'

'I can't believe it either,' I said.

'It's terrible.'

'That's an understatement. Imagine thinking you were going to have a lovely experience in nature, you know, relatively safe and everything, and then you die?'

'And what did that guy on the pier say, they put her in a ... *bag*?' my mother-in-law said, the hint of laughter in her voice.

'I'm picturing like a vomit bag,' I said, 'one of those ones the stewards were handing round.'

'I spewed in one!' she exclaimed. 'I've never done that before!'

'We went whale watching and all we got was a near-death experience!'

'We went whale watching and all we got was vomit on our shoes!'

We were really laughing now. The children had run ahead, racing each other to the car. My mother-in-law was cackling and it felt good to laugh after the awful journey we'd just shared. 'We went whale watching and we didn't even see a whale!' I said.

'No,' said my mother-in-law, wiping tears of laughter from her eyes. 'We didn't even see a fucking whale.'

Up ahead, the girls were waiting by the car. My mother-in-law's looks were definitely improved. I wanted to tell her that I was sorry for being unsympathetic to her struggles, and sometimes doubting the veracity of her stories. My mother-in-law, I realised, just wanted me to understand her. She was trying to communicate, in her particular way.

Instead I said, 'I'm glad you're feeling better, Vicky. I'm really, really glad.'

The wind nagged at my collar as I clipped my daughters into their seats. When we were back on the road, the girls content once more to play on their devices, my mother-in-law asked quietly if I took any pictures of us to send to Al. I told her I'd forgotten – with the wind and rain, the spray, the waves and then the chaos in the cabin, taking photos had completely slipped my mind.

'Oh well,' she said. 'Maybe we don't tell him what really happened.'

'What do you mean?'

'All Alex wants to know is that we had a good time. If the two of us said to him, Al, the tour was cut short because the sea was so rough that somebody died, we didn't even get to see a whale, I vomited in a bag, I thought I was going to pass out, you looked like you were about to have a panic attack, and so on, he would only get upset. You know what he's like; too many details put him off. And then he'll say we're being dramatic or complain about the expense or feel obliged to make us feel better about our failure, he'll spend all this time researching the best whale watching spots and planning another trip and it will become this huge thing. So maybe … yeah. Maybe we don't tell him what really happened.'

I glanced from the road to my mother-in-law. 'Do you mean we should lie, or … ?

'I mean there's no harm in editing the story.'

She was wearing a sly little smile and I felt a similar emotion tugging at the corners of my mouth. 'Get out my phone,' I instructed.

For all my husband knew we had seen a peduncle slap, and it blew our fucking minds.

THE MARTINI EFFECT

T HEY SHARED A BIRTHDAY – Jane and the woman who was going to deliver her baby. It was November but she wasn't due until March.

Sundi was a white woman about ten years older than Jane, originally from the Northern Rivers. She was small and doughy, with fine red hair and so many freckles that they joined to form a splodgy tan. The gifts she brought were those your stoner housemates might have coveted, like stubs of Palo Santo, small organic chocolates and daily affirmations. Predictably her food was of the kind that dried out in the bain-maries of health food shops in coastal towns throughout the nineties, and Jane had to get used to eating seaweed, rice balls, fried tempeh and tuna patties whenever they met up. She was the most earnest embodiment of a stereotype Jane had ever met, which was seductive and embarrassing in equal measure. The point was, Sundi made her feel as though she had decided to do something important.

Jane had chosen her to be her doula based on recommendations from a couple of her friends, whose natural births had been, in their words, the most visceral and ecstatic moments of their lives. Personality-wise, Sundi was eccentric though knowledgeable and basically likeable, even if she was an oversharer. Maybe that's what made her likeable – despite her quirks you couldn't help but feel affection for her, knowing all you did about her life.

That they shared a birthday sealed it: coincidence, especially in times of adjustment, can often look like fate.

On their birthday, Sundi called to ask if she could come around. 'It's a big deal, your first birthday as a life-giving mother. We should celebrate.'

Jane hesitated a moment before agreeing, but the prospect of spending her birthday alone was depressing and Sundi's company was better than none. There was a part of her, too, that wondered which details of her life Sundi would impart on such a special occasion, and whether they might resonate with Jane's own situation. Now that she was in her second trimester, the reality of her condition was impossible to deny. She felt the precarity pressing down upon her and could do with some advice.

These were the facts: she was pregnant and she hadn't said a word about it to Romil.

Oh, Romil!

In her mind lately he was partying with a group of stylish, arrogant Danes who were definitely fucking him. She had lain in bed this morning picturing him in Copenhagen, where he had gone to learn how to make petit fours under the tutelage of a world-class pastry chef, walking by a still canal on his way back from the kitchen, linked in with an icy blonde, wearing the scarf she'd given him as a going-away present right before he said he couldn't see long-distance working for them, after all.

That he was capable of cruelty, she knew – there had been glimpses of it during their relationship. She could hear it in the way he spoke about people, even their closest friends. He was uncompromising, and he did not believe he should explain himself to anyone. He did what he wanted and he didn't tell you why.

In the weeks after their break-up, Jane had tried to talk to him. 'Please,' she begged, 'I don't understand.'

'I know,' he said.

'But you don't care.'

Romil was still, as still as a monument. He was standing in the doorframe and she was hunched up on the floor, her back to their bed, crying. There was nothing in his face – no feeling. She couldn't read him. All he said was, 'I don't have anything to say.'

The last time she messaged him was to ask why he had called her in the middle of the night.

Sorry, pocket call, Romil replied.

It hurt her all over and she cried.

It didn't seem to bother Sundi that Jane never talked about the father, it being her belief that dads were secondary and in fact dispensable where babies were concerned. Jane thought she must agree with this to some extent, otherwise she wouldn't be here, but she'd decided long ago that she would do it with Romil, an idea that proved hard to relinquish. It had been almost five months. She was going to tell him, honestly; she was waiting for a good time.

WHEN SUNDI ARRIVED, SHE slapped her bag down on the table and then placed her hands directly on Jane's belly. 'Hello, sweet Energy,' she said, which was what she called the baby. 'How are you growing today?'

'Okay, I think,' said Jane.

'And what about you, Mumma? How are you feeling?'

She winced and turned away so Sundi wouldn't see her face. At first it had bothered her – *Mumma* – but Jane had given up trying to resist it. This was one of her biggest problems: she had no energy for anything. She was neither passionate nor ambivalent, the maintenance of which she found too hard. Instead she let things happen to her, and it was only later, carried by the current of what was already in motion, that she questioned her decisions knowing that the opportunity to change things had definitely passed.

'Will you have tea?' she asked now.

'I've got something better,' said Sundi, drawing from her bag a four-pack of brightly coloured cans. 'Martinis,' she explained. 'They're actually not bad. Let's have one.'

'I shouldn't,' said Jane.

'Oh, they're fine; they're organic and non-alcoholic.'

Jane got a glass out of the cupboard, which Sundi filled halfway. It was fizzy and tasted a bit like burger pickles, but it was alright. She thought about Romil again and how martinis were tradition on her birthday. Sundi had known this somehow. It was all so strange.

'What am I going to do?' she asked suddenly.

'Soon enough that baby is going to decide for you,' said Sundi matter-of-factly. 'So it doesn't really matter what you do. Anyway, you might surprise yourself. You might do something completely unexpected.'

Sundi drifted toward the couch, where lozenges of sunlight fell upon her and dissolved. It was one of those calm, fresh spring days. Jane, sitting on the other couch, sensed Sundi gearing up for some great revelation and she waited attentively, willing to find meaning in whatever she described, a family holiday where she and her sisters joined their father at a tiny island on the Great Barrier Reef. Neil – that was his name – had planned the trip and paid for all their tickets, but it was not without trepidation that they boarded the ferry that day.

It was a while ago now, said Sundi, when she and her sisters were all in their twenties; her youngest sister Sunny must have been very young, barely out of her teens. It was preternaturally bright and chilly in the sun, the first of that day's jarring qualities. Sunny had a migraine and was lying in the ferry terminal with a hat over her eyes. Samira, the middle child, was hungover and coming down from a festival in Byron Bay. There had been an issue with their tickets and they missed the ferry connection, which was non-refundable; they'd had to pay a premium and had been waiting hours for the next one. Sitting in the bright, cold sunlight, Sundi went to put her sunglasses on and realised she had left them on the plane. It was one of those mornings, she observed, in which every small failure is a prelude to disaster.

Neil had flown up earlier from his house in Adelaide, which meant they could expect to find him at the resort when they arrived. As the ferry charged through choppy waters on its way toward the island, Sundi's apprehension mounted. She felt seasick and went inside. Sunny was hunched over by a window.

'Why are we doing this?' she asked.

'Because,' said Sundi.

And they both knew it would be the last of these trips before he died.

Neil was a difficult man to be around, said Sundi, even before he started dying. He was depressive and unstable, married to a bitterness he let spill over and spoil different parts of his life. Even so, he did not want it to end. 'I didn't understand him. He complained incessantly – since I was a kid I'd been hearing him talk about how easy it would be to kill himself, how he would like to die. He could be so bitter and resentful, I thought he hated life.' But now she thought that Neil's resentment showed how passionate he was about living, and it was only with his diagnosis, which he often referred to as a 'death sentence,' that life became significant. 'Maybe it's like that old saying: we hate what we love most.'

Jane, who had finished her small taste of the martini, got up to make some tea. It seemed to startle Sundi and she leapt up, holding her can in front of her like she'd been caught. 'Is this too much? Let me know if I'm oversharing.'

'No,' said Jane, 'keep going.' She was beginning to feel that gentle, soothing indifference she always got when someone else took control of a situation. 'I'm listening,' she said, lying back on the other couch as Sundi continued with her story.

The island had its place in family mythology. Back in the sixties, Neil had wound up there on his way to the Whitsundays, where he scuba dived with some Torres Strait Islanders, camped on the beach and got washed out by a storm. Wanting to relive the romance of his first encounter, he took them there when they were kids, right before their parents' separation. As the harbour came into view, Sundi was awash with memories of crystal water, dripping vegetation, the reef shark's black-tipped tail. Making friends with a girl at the pool, retirees on the day beds, a skinny guy who played jazz standards in the restaurant every night. Her dad accused her mum of looking at him. Yes – another thing – the silences. The way her parents fought without saying much at all.

It was a radical place, she told Jane, small enough to circumnavigate in an hour and incredibly biodiverse, home to thousands of species of marine invertebrates, fish, mammals, plants, nesting turtles, and in the summer months, over two hundred thousand seabirds. It was the shearwaters she remembered, nesting in their thousands all over the island.

Everything was covered in their shit, and the dense briny smell of them was second only to the incessant noise which woke her family early in the morning and kept them up at night. During the long hours before sunrise she would hear her parents' ugly whispers, and knew that in the morning they would not look each other in the eye.

One day while roaming around the forest near their villa, Sundi came upon a pair of shearwaters guarding a large, broken egg. The birds looked distraught, she said, protecting their egg with weary vigilance, as though they were in mourning. She turned and ran and after that avoided going back there; it was not until years later that she read that shearwaters are monogamous and will only divorce if a breeding season fails. Her fear of them was, she realised, an early intimation of her parents' separation – which she intuited for the first time on seeing those grieving birds.

'You don't need a degree in psychology to see how it affected me,' Sundi laughed, self-deprecatingly. 'I'm still trying to save that fucking egg.'

'I have a degree in psychology,' said Jane. 'And now I work at a supermarket.'

'Checks out,' Sundi said.

Jane couldn't bring herself to laugh.

'Anyway,' went Sundi, 'as we got off the ferry I got a spooky sense of déjà vu. I knew that just like last time, something bad was going to happen.'

'Why did you go? I mean, besides the obvious, why go there in the first place if you knew it was going to be awful?'

'That's just what we did with him. We answered when he called.'

All those times that Neil had threatened to kill himself had made them vigilant, she explained. 'He would break down and cry and then he would be happy again, playing guitar and dancing, telling us these crazy stories after school.' It was confusing. They stopped believing he would really do it, but they still felt responsible for him in ways that children ought not to feel. When he was given a prognosis it was momentarily relieving; her father's life, she said, was not her responsibility anymore.

They left the pier and got directions to their room. Immediately it started raining, an intense tropical downpour which soaked their clothes as Sundi and her sisters dragged their luggage through the rainforest. She thought about her dad and how he'd start complaining just as soon as they arrived; he had always been vocal about his problems without ever doing the slightest thing about them. Her apprehension gave way to something more dispiriting. His cancer had been long and painful, going on for many years, and now that he had a real reason to complain Sundi found herself resenting it even more, his suffering and whatever obliged her to keep witnessing.

'After all he'd put us through as kids, I was pissed off with him for rubbing it in my face. I bet that sounds terrible.'

'I don't know,' murmured Jane.

Sundi barely heard her. 'When he opened the door,' she continued, 'the first thing I thought was that he looked insane. He had always been a little mad but now he looked different, as if the scales had finally tipped. His hair was all crazy and white, longer than I'd ever seen it, and his expression was turned inward. It's hard to explain, but it seemed like he was seeing something very different to what was real for us. I think the right word is uncanny. His face was like a haunted house.'

For the first few days it poured with rain; they rarely left the villa. Sundi and her sisters played cards and read, trying to ignore Neil's ceaseless chatter, which seemed to echo round the villa like the nattering, squawking, shrilling noises of the seabirds. After a while the two streams of sound became indistinguishable, and Sundi had the impression that her dad had lost some of his human qualities: an impression that was heightened by the fact that with his fluffy white hair, large nose and prominent black monobrow, Neil intensely resembled an albatross.

'The place got really messy. Dad put a picture of his Indian guru on top of the stereo, like that was going to calm things down. He started talking to us in this crazy way; I would ask if we should go down to breakfast,' she explained, 'and he would say, *Why does the bee drink from the flower?*'

'Why *does* the bee drink from the flower?'

'Yeah. I don't fucking know.'

Just as it had been before, he kept them all awake at night, ranting about nonsensical things or repeating lines of poetry, and if they begged for quiet he would look at them, his eyes gleaming in the darkness, a gleam she did not see so much as sense, and reply, *You ask me how to find peace. I ask you, what is peace?*

This was kind of normal, this manner of speaking – something he had learned as a disciple of the guru – so it was hard to tell whether it was really unusual, a new eccentricity to worry over, or just another of Neil's strange ways of loving and teaching them lessons. 'It is my responsibility as a father,' he kept saying, 'to show you the way before I die.'

After days of this the women left the room to walk the length of the island. The unceasing rain had soaked the white sand to a fine clay and the whole reef was obscured beneath reflected cloud. Sundi thought of Neil's continued dominion over her and her sisters, all of them now adults, and decided it depended precisely on his speaking this way. That is, his tyranny relied on his never making sense.

Jane was becoming excited. The way Sundi described her dad was reminiscent of a paper she had read by D.W. Winnicott, right before she abandoned her PhD, which offered for analysis the case of a mother who kept her children in a state of organised chaos. Eagerly, she explained to Sundi how the mother broke everything into fragments, their whole life, battering her children with a constant stream of argument and entertainment, all of it designed to distract from the real trouble, the mother's sense that she was coming loose from herself.

Sundi, who was becoming agitated too, said, 'At one point he was singing songs from an old musical and it dawned on me that he was not singing the lyrics I knew.

I suddenly doubted whether the lyrics I knew were the real lyrics, or if it was actually me who had been singing them wrong all along.' She felt severely dislocated from her sense of the facts; he tended to have this effect.

After five days the rain stopped. The island dried out slowly, releasing the perfume of tropical flowers, the tang of salt water and the oily white stink of guano. When they went outside everything seemed surreal, too fresh and sparkling and bright. Neil slept for fifteen hours, she said, and woke again restored.

'But this was even more disturbing than the madness,' she explained. They had no idea how long it would last and if the return of his faculties was legitimate or just another phase of his delirium. They kept vigilant, watching for changes in his mood.

In the meantime, he wanted to scuba dive. It was the last opportunity he'd have before he died. There's nothing like gliding high above the sea floor in the current, Neil said; the quiet, the view, the total weightlessness. It was the closest man came to flying. The way he described it sounded beautiful, but not trusting him to go alone, between themselves the sisters elected Sundi to do the refresher course with him, which ran for three days in the tepid green expanse of the resort's saltwater pool.

Sundi was apprehensive, but during their hours in the pool Neil behaved wonderfully, listening to the instructor quietly and telling, where appropriate, genial stories of his forays underwater. He got the knack of it quickly, his muscle memory returning, and the instructor permitted him to scull around the pool freely while the others struggled with masks and tanks and hand signals, which were numerous and somehow the hardest part for her to grasp.

In the pool, said Sundi, it was hard not to think of herself as acting among the sunbathing retirees and honeymooning couples and the kids jumping in and out. When she tried to imagine what it would be like to actually leave the pool and dive beyond the safety of the reef, she drew a blank. It was all darkness. She was frightened of the unknown. The closer they got to the assessment, the more she found herself wishing the course would never end.

Neil, on the other hand, knew everything. When the instructor explained the risks of surfacing too fast he nodded his head vigorously. The bends, he said – I saw it happen to a friend. When the instructor told them that descending below sixty metres could amount to feeling drunk, nitrogen working on the body's cells like a narcotic, Neil's hand shot up like a kid in class. They call it *rapture of the deep*, he told his course-mates – also known as the Martini Effect.

As the course progressed toward the final assessment, Sundi started freaking out. She knew that Neil would do something erratic and she didn't feel capable of keeping them safe. Her sisters told her to pay attention to the training so if something happened, she would know how to respond.

On the final afternoon of the course they were each to be tested in the pool. Her dad went in confidently, and as she watched him move through the sequence they'd been taught, Sundi thought that she had never seen him so clearly. She was moved by his determination and grace, while at the same time she was furious, incensed by the very things she admired. It seemed unfair that he would present such poise and unity of character to the outside world when she and her sisters only ever saw him breaking up.

After she too had passed her test, the instructor let them practice in the pool and Neil began criticising her technique. He was particularly annoyed about her hand signals and wanted to demonstrate them correctly. She watched him go through the sequence again, mirroring the shapes he made with his fingers, while a violent fantasy overcame her. Instead of making the sign for 'okay' she saw herself rip the mouthpiece from his lips, put her hands around his neck and hold him underwater. She almost felt him thrashing, could anticipate the moment when the struggle went from his body and the water would be calm. The vision frightened her. She made an excuse and got out.

The day of their dive arrived and with it the first real sun. The cloudless sky was so blue it looked two-dimensional, like a picture of itself. Below them was the water and the luminous coral reef, and as they sped toward the drop-off point Sundi imagined unlocking its wonders, understood her dad's excitement and began to feel some of her own.

At the edge of the reef each diver strode off the side. She evacuated the water from her mask as she'd been taught, but when she opened her eyes she was confronted with a chilling vision: spreading out before her was not the life she had imagined but an endless, formless blue. The entire seascape was blanched of colour, as if the effort to appear vivid from above had caused a total blandness below. She swam around in search of the reef's magic but was disappointed. Why am I doing this? she wondered, drifting limply at Neil's side.

The instructor had been adamant that they should always remain within eyesight of their buddy. But as they approached the bommie, Neil saw something interesting and shot off in pursuit. As she had predicted, he had done something erratic; she saw his fins churning water, bubbles exploded in her face. He disappeared around the back of the immense formation and she followed after him in panic. She circled the bommie once and then again, but he was gone.

Remembering her training she stopped, established neutral buoyancy and spun three-sixty degrees. She looked above and below, trying to spot his bubbles. As she turned her body slowly in the water, a strange calm overcame her. Her father had put them both in danger, but in a way, she felt that he had finally released her from responsibility. She could not save him. She understood that nothing she did mattered; she did not have to be vigilant anymore. It was like that first big moment of relief when he got his diagnosis: an immense burden had lifted, now it was out of her hands.

Just then Neil swam up from beneath her. He was frantically signalling, although she couldn't interpret what his hands were trying to say. Once they were back in the boat, he ripped off his mask and began jabbering excitedly about giant clams and sea turtles, about an octopus which shot its inky serum in his face, about parrotfish and clownfish and a manta ray the size of a car, a tale of triumph which quickly turned into an attack on Sundi, whose inability to get out of her head, in Neil's words, prevented her from noticing what had been there all along. A familiar rage swelled within her and she let herself be harnessed by it, rising to the crest of its wave. 'It felt so good,' she said, 'to finally give in.'

When she regained a sense of herself, Neil was whimpering on the floor of the charter boat and she was standing over him, still dripping, the sensation of his slender neck prickling on her palms.

'You strangled him?' Jane asked incredulously.

'I don't remember,' she said. And then, 'I once saw a large dog, a Rottweiler, throttle our Jack Russel, shaking his limp body from side to side. I felt like the Rottweiler. All these people rushed to our side of the boat and someone must have bumped me because I lost my footing and the next second I was in.'

Underneath, it was quiet. The water was unimaginably soft. The blue was all around her again and the boat somewhere above, for she could hear footfalls reverberate as people moved around inside. She was dimly aware, after the adrenaline had passed, that she had gone overboard, though again she felt completely calm. For a while she floated, devoid of urgency. Then she kicked, pulled, and surfaced into brilliant light.

'On the way back to the island, I was stunned. Later I would feel ashamed, but the thing I felt right then was just this sense of an event. Something had happened, changing the course of things. You have to understand that the violence in our house had been the violence of Dad's preferences, the agony of his despair, the intensity of his love. It was damaging, but it wasn't physical. I hadn't known that I was capable of hurting him, only that I'd often wanted to do something to make him stop. It took an unexpected form – strangling him was such an outrageous reaction that my sisters and I still laugh about it, but it was obviously disturbing. And it didn't produce any special revelations. Instead it complicated everything, because now I had to reckon with my own violence and aggression, as well as the guilt and pain.'

'Did you ever speak with him about it?'

'I wrote him a letter which I don't know if he read. Not long after we got back from the island he went into palliative care, and then a few weeks later, he died.'

They were silent for a moment in which Sundi drank and Jane did not know what to say. She was thinking of that phrase, the Martini Effect – blood aspirated with noxious gases, death disguised as drunkenness. It was so hard to distinguish between a good thing and a bad thing, or to know which one you'd choose. What was the point of it all? She was about to ask what she thought when Sundi finished her canned martini, stood up and said that she should go.

As Jane said goodbye and let her out onto the street, Sundi gave her a hug. Resting her head on her shoulder, she sighed.

'Don't worry,' said Sundi, patting her on the back. 'You're lucky – everything is moving beautifully.'

After she left, Jane sat in the courtyard where she lapsed into a dull, uncertain reverie. It was still her birthday, a nice afternoon. She was almost five months pregnant, she still hadn't told Romil and despite her willingness to be moved, nothing seemed profoundly different. Sundi's story had been interesting, but it was not really important. As she thought this, Jane felt very lonely.

Just then, the baby moved and startled her. Why am I doing this? she asked herself once more. The courtyard had grown chilly. Because, she thought, well ... and after a while drew her cardigan around herself and went inside.

BRINK MAN

ACT I

After a lull in his career, Jack stages a comeback. He applies for a residency down at Point Nepean, accepts the offer of a cottage with no stipend, packs his laptop, notebooks, novels, whisky, wine, some meagre foodstuffs and a pouch of rolling tobacco with a little green mixed in and leaves, one sunny afternoon in August, for the coast.

The inner and then outer suburbs roll away beneath his tyres. He passes Frankston, Dromana, Rye. Overtaking an elderly couple towing a caravan he catches sight of his reflection in the rear-view mirror; his fine brow and silver hair which falls to just below his ears. His teeth are nice, his eyes are sparkling and his wrinkles are the kind you get from reading, typing and formulating big ideas; in his opinion, they make him look refined. At the age of sixty-nine he is still attractive. He has the energy, the aura of a younger man.

Jack drives his Subaru Forrester quickly, pushing the speed limit. There is agitation mounting in his body – he jigs his leg, drums his fingers on the steering wheel. Although the current running from his head to chest to navel isn't exactly sexual it's not *not* sexual, a youthful feeling, one belonging to the rush of years when life was about women and poetry and getting things for free.

He thinks of the women in his life to date, or at least those women whom he feels were most significant. His Nanna, bless her, whose granny flat he would retreat to after school. His daughters, now in their late twenties, each with a life of her own. His first love Kate. The girls' mother Diana, whom he left for Sarah after fifteen years of marriage, Sarah being twenty-five years younger and the hit of oxygen he thought he needed. When Sarah left him in her turn he soothed his broken ego by pursuing a tumultuous affair with Fiona Phelan, beloved TV personality and total narcissist; their time together was brief but its impact was profound.

He leans back in the driver's seat, admiring his list. It is not exhaustive, but it represents important phases of his life. For better or worse, he has learned more from these women than from any other source. If, at times, he has wondered whether his career would not have benefited from his being less preoccupied with sex and matters of the heart, he reminds himself that his relationships – getting into them, falling out of them – are still the most convincing education he's received.

Just then a cloud, crossing the sun, throws the Forrester into shadow, forcing him to think about another woman he does not wish to acknowledge. Her name alone is enough to produce a painful feeling. With some effort, he puts her from his mind.

Far better to think of Elizabeth, the lawyer he's been seeing for the past couple of years. He is fond of her – she is candid, switched on and sexually exciting. Last week she encouraged him to go down on her during her lunch break, in her office chair. The chair swivelled every time he applied a different pressure to her clitoris. It was hard to get any traction, but still Elizabeth moaned. The sweaty fragrance of her cunt put him in mind of boardroom meetings, skirts and stockings, legs pressed together under tables, the rush of the evening commute. If he is honest, her career arouses him. He and Diana struggled to raise a family on their artists' wages, and there is something encouraging in the security – even if it's only speculative – attached to Elizabeth and her job.

At forty-seven some would say she's young for him, but as Diana remarked when she first heard, as Jack has gotten older the women appear to have gotten younger. Diana meant to embarrass him, as though Jack should admit that he's a tired old cliché, but notwithstanding the respect he has for his ex-wife, he doesn't bore himself with other people's standards. He believes in the complexity of his desire, and he is fundamentally uninterested in the morality of today.

On the outskirts of Sorrento, he calls Elizabeth's mobile and listens to the dial tone ring out. It crosses his mind that she is trying to ignore him. Undeterred, he calls again. This time she answers on the second ring.

'I'm driving and I'm horny. Tell me something good,' he says, half in jest, realising too late that Elizabeth's seven-year-old daughter Grace has answered the phone.

'Grace,' he stumbles, 'hello. Is your mum around?'

'Um,' says Grace.

He can hear Elizabeth talking in the background. 'Can you put her on please?'

There are muffled, static sounds as the phone is passed into a different pair of hands. Then Elizabeth's voice says, 'What?'

'I'm thinking about you.'

'Why?'

'About this morning. Before I left, I should have made you come.'

Elizabeth pauses. 'I see you've recovered from last night. You didn't say anything weird to Grace, did you?'

'Of course not. What the hell.'

'So you're feeling better? That's good.' He hears her walk into another room. 'You got an email from uni – something about a memorial morning tea.'

'Why were you looking at my email?'

'I don't know, you left it logged in. It just popped up when I went to use my computer. Sorry. Whose funeral is it, anyway?'

'Someone in the faculty – it doesn't matter. Listen, I'm driving. I have to go.'

Jack accelerates again, spurred on by annoyance. It is not just because Elizabeth has perved on his emails; he is suddenly offended by the whole world. The geriatric couple in the caravan. The administration at the university where he is a doctoral candidate. Diana with her moral high ground, pronouncing her post-menopausal judgements on his life. Why are people so obsessed with scrutinising other people? Jack likes to think that he is different. Live and let live.

His worst scorn is reserved for the critics who canned his last play. This was a few years ago now, and Jack has not written since. In the past his shows would get a sell-out run, but though the season started well, by closing night they'd struggled to fill seats. Apparently, people were too afraid of censure to appreciate political satire. This had upset him on a personal level, but more so because it proved his suspicion that art has re-entered a grim age of censorship and denial. He thinks of some reviews, indelibly sketched on his mind:

Merely interesting ★★★

A trite commentary which fails to hit the mark ★★

Left us wondering whether veteran playwright
Jack Halliday is past it ★★

Does this play, for all its brass and bluster, advance
a transgressive politics? Is it even accurate to say it is
political? Halliday's latest production is one more

> *example of "provocative" theatre which masks its*
> *narrow-mindedness by satisfying consumer expecta-*
> *tions about diversity* ★

Fuck the lot of 'em, thinks Jack. In his younger days he truly believed that artists and critics could achieve a mutually sustaining relationship. When he received bad reviews, he tried his best to mend his ways. Aren't we all anxious to improve ourselves, once we know how and where to improve? Most criticism now he finds empty, a reflex. He does not believe their impressions of him are accurate or true and so resents their asking him to change.

Passing Portsea, he allows his frustration to become righteous. He is sick of being misapprehended, and he has wasted too much time in hiding. By the end of this residency, he vows, there will be another script.

The road narrows to a single lane and then the houses drop away. He takes the turn-off to the national park, where he will stay for the next two weeks. An information point or two describes the historical significance of the area to both the Bunurong people and the settler colony, but Jack does not stop or get out of the car to read them. Perhaps it is better to abandon politics, he thinks. Maybe this time he'll go mainstream with a screenplay about something iconic, a women's prison or a bikie gang or a rape set in rural NSW. His critics won't know what hit them. He will show them he's back from the brink.

THE SUN FLARES AND then drops low on the horizon, and everything blazes gold. Heading seaward, he passes through a coastal wood of windswept grasses pricked with banksia, sheoakes and Moonah trees. He sees no one. It is not far out of town but nonetheless it feels remote, a landscape touched by nothing but the light.

The cottage is part of an ex-colonial compound on a cliff above the sea. It is capital-R Romantic, invoking the richness of a costume drama: Lord Byron, the piano forte, men on horseback, a virgin ravished in a greenhouse in the rain. The reality is far less glamorous. The cottages were built to house the families of policemen who patrolled here in the 1850s, when a vast quarantine station operated at the point. Jack thinks of these men, whose job it would have been to apprehend illegal goods and sickly immigrants who had been tossed up on the shore. Their labour was restrictive, not creative – much like the critics he despises. It pleases him to think that he is not one of their kind.

There is no reception on his phone and then the cottages look empty when they first come into view. He recalls his contact telling him, in an email, that he would be the only artist staying there. At first it disappointed him to know he'd be alone, but now he's looking forward to the solitude. These days he spends most of his time at Elizabeth's – he is basically living there – and although he finds it comfortable, he is keen to occupy a space where no one can distract him from his task.

Elizabeth was not convinced. 'Solitude's not really your thing,' she'd said last night. 'Those cottages are definitely haunted.'

He snorted. 'Sure.'

'Look at them!' Jack leaned over her to get a better look at the screen. The weatherboard cottage in the photos had a red tin roof, a sloping verandah and tiny little windows chalked with minerals and spray. There was a front yard bordered by a lavender hedge, a bay tree, a brick chimney, an outhouse, a low wide porch and two cane chairs slumped side by side.

'What's wrong with it?' he asked. 'It looks completely fine!'

'It looks completely fucking haunted. Look at those chairs on the verandah! Some sick old sadist probably died in one while wanking over his dead mother.'

'As a trope, Elizabeth, that one's been overdone.'

Yet it was true that there was something sad and empty about those chairs, the careless way they'd been arranged.

'Can't it just be an old building, without being full of guilty consciences and ghosts?'

Elizabeth scrolled through the photos again. 'I thought you'd be inspired by all of that stuff. You can just imagine what went on there.'

'Yes, but see you're failing to distinguish between what's real and what's imaginary.'

She was silent before closing her browser. 'I wasn't asking for a lecture.'

All that evening, he thought about ghosts. He did not believe in them, except as a theatrical device. He was not about to buy into the Gothic-settler mythscape, like so many other artists. Like he said, it was not the most original theme. Preoccupied with these thoughts, he was silent over dinner. Elizabeth let him sulk. But when they went to bed she sucked his cock and right before he came she fucked his arsehole with her fingers and because of this his orgasm pierced him like an arrow and he cried out suddenly, as if he had been shot.

Elizabeth straddled him playfully. 'What's wrong. Wait. Is something actually wrong? What are you doing, are you crying?'

He lay beneath her, wrung out and depleted, struck by a sudden, unbearable grief.

'I'm worried about you,' she went on. 'Since Paris, you've been ... I don't know. Something's changed.'

'Mum,' he heard Grace calling from the other room. '*Muuuuuuuuuuuum.*'

Elizabeth looked down at him and swept his hair back from his face. 'Hold on. I'll just go and get her back to sleep.'

'Mum!' the child's voice was verging on hysterical.

'She's had another bad dream.'

'Would you just go and shut her up?' he snapped.

He tried to sit up, but Elizabeth was crushing him. 'GET THE FUCK OFF ME!' he shrieked, pushing her off and fleeing to the bathroom, where he sat on the toilet and sobbed until she finally knocked on the door.

'Jack?' she said gently.

'Fuck off Elizabeth, I'm fine!' he shrieked.

'You don't seem fine. Are you okay? Do you want to tell me what's going on?'

'Stop scrutinising me. It's an unattractive habit.'

He heard her sighing through the door. 'Fucking hell. I never know where the edge is with you.'

HE PUNCHES A CODE into the lockbox and retrieves the keys. The door unlocks with a little click which sounds too loud and he is greeted by a rush of stale air. Stepping over the threshold, he has the distinct sense that he's intruding on someone else's space. He half expects to meet them in the hallway, but there is nothing but a creepy credenza stacked with ancient books, ornaments and faded, broken shells.

Inside the cottage it is freezing. He goes around switching on lights, trying to dispel the impression that the place looks like a halfway house where someone down and out might go for refuge from injustice, boyfriends, poverty or meth. There is lino on almost every surface. The furniture is mismatched and often leaning to one side.

Worse still are the traces of past residents in every room: the pantry cluttered with half-empty sachets of pasta, the microwaveable trays of stroganoff and butter chicken growing stalagmites in the freezer, as dispiriting now as the day they were bought. The bedroom has the sweet, musky smell of a woman, and there is a dirty make-up wipe smeared with lipstick and concealer in a corner of the bathroom, beneath the sink. He shudders. It is just the kind of detail women always miss.

Jack wrinkles his nose, picturing the resident before him. He imagines she was a poet, and not a very good one. The childish painting in the loungeroom of a demented owl with large, unblinking eyes was probably left there by her kid. The whole thing is really unpalatable and somehow makes him think of Grace's night terrors; he used to have them too. It should make him compassionate, but she is always waking up in the night and getting into their bed.

Elizabeth says it's just a phase. She says that Grace has an overactive imagination and wonders if that means she'll become some kind of artist.

'I don't know why she has them. I've never had nightmares; I don't even remember my dreams. But then I'm so left-brained! Completely analytical. Did you have them as a kid?'

'No,' Jack lies. 'Maybe. I don't remember. But creativity doesn't have to be anti-rational. I'm fairly sensible, am I not?'

This seems to amuse her.

'What's funny?' he asks.

'Nothing,' she smiles. 'You definitely have a certain *sensibility*. You're quite emotional. It's refreshing in a man of your generation.'

Yes – he has artistic sensibilities. Ferrying his belongings from the car, Jack tries to reframe his situation. His lodgings may be cheap, ugly and uncomfortable, but there are stories in these walls. Ignoring the owl, he places his hand on the chilly plaster and tries to channel a few characters. Sadistic coppers. Smugglers. Diseased immigrants. Trapped and hardened colonial wives. Sickly children, the dead and dying, the Bunurong women who were tricked and stolen from the point by Dutch sealers, the Dutch sealers themselves, stinking drunk and covered in blood. He could have a lot of fun with them. They are not happy stories, but when did drama give a shit about a happy ending?

Eager to see the writing space, he goes into the study. There is a fireplace in the corner boarded up with random sheets of MDF and yet another broken chair against the writing desk. The desk itself is large and wide, its surface marred by chips and scratches, biro marks and coffee rings. He sits down, trying to imagine writing a new play or working on his doctoral thesis, but he's distracted by a piece of graffiti. Putting on his glasses, he bends to read it.

A writer is never alone.

Why would someone write that? Disquieted, he closes the door to that room.

THE AFTERNOON DIMINISHES AND evening comes on darkly. Wind howls around the cottage, rattling the windowpanes and making leaves scratch on the glass. Somewhere in the house a door is banging, but despite several laps he cannot find the banging's source. He sets up his things in the bedroom, kitchen and study, fighting disappointment.

He contemplates sending the council an email to complain about the situation – *hardly conducive to creative labour!* – but the fight goes out of him before he's even filled the subject field. Defeated, he rolls himself a cigarette and pours a glass of wine.

With the wine in one hand and his ciggie in the other, he goes outside to smoke on the verandah. The other chair sits empty and he longs for company, Elizabeth or his daughters, who would know how to make the situation light. He types a message to their group chat before remembering about the reception. 'Fucking shithole,' he swears, tossing his phone to one side.

His gaze meets the horizon. The wind has blown some wispy cirrus clouds across the cliffs and in the last dregs of the light he contemplates their strange formations. Their hairiness reminds him of the prize-winning Afghan hound his father kept when he was a boy, a strange pet for a family in 1960s Seaford. Exhaling a plume of smoke, he permits himself a shudder. He hates the memory of this dog.

Sighthounds are incredibly neurotic – even the slightest shift in household dynamics will upset them – and discovering this, his older brother Graham bullied it. Jack went along with Graham's antics until he could no longer stomach the dog's distress, second only to their father's, who almost had a nervous breakdown over the abuse. But Jack remembers being embarrassed, even after they had stopped harassing it, not only by the Afghan hound's audacious looks. He was ashamed of his father's overzealous affection for the spoiled, sensitive animal – for it did not seem like the sort of thing a man should love.

Both dog and dad are long dead, and Jack fell out with Graham years ago. Diana always used to say that it should bother him, but Jack maintains that it does not. Relationships end – he is well aware – for various reasons, and however much they've taught you, there is no point hanging onto them once they're done.

He goes inside and pours himself another glass of wine, thinking that he's satisfied with this assessment. But as he makes a simple meal of vegetables and rice, he can't help repeating the words graffitied on the desk. *A writer is never alone.* He thinks of what he said to Elizabeth yesterday and how he wanted to pretend that people, like houses, are not always filled with guilty consciences and ghosts. Because it strikes him now that he is often plagued by memories and uneasiness regarding others – Diana, Sarah, his father, Graham – even that bloody dog. Others who have wronged him, or whom he has wronged.

Since Paris it is Hannah.

He tries to forget her, but he cannot keep her from his mind.

ACT II

They met when he was in his late forties and Hannah was twenty-two. He was enjoying a successful run at the box office and she was a shy intern working for the production company putting on his play: a work of political satire taking down the United States of Bush. The critics were calling it *essential*. America had just invaded Iraq.

Hannah had been hired to do something but nobody knew what it was. The word that came to mind was *useless*. She was timid and always found lurking – literally – in the wings. Even her looks grated on him, her frightened face and long, fine hair which hung self-consciously about her head. When you talked to her she seemed to tremble. She reminded him – yes – she reminded him of his father's Afghan hound.

Jack preferred a more boisterous type of woman. He was just famous enough to be flirted with by all the glossy little actresses coming in and out of dressing rooms, girls who knew what it felt like to be wanted. He didn't pay her much attention until she arrived on opening night wearing lipstick in a shocking shade of red. It was totally incongruous with her personality, but Jack found himself saying, 'Your lipstick … it suits you.'

Hannah widened her eyes and said, 'Oh.'

When he saw her again at interval, it was clear she'd gone somewhere and wiped it off. He pictured the smear of red on white tissue and a distant thrill went through him. For the first time since they'd met, Hannah seemed like a woman with whom he could have an affair. But he was worried he had frightened her.

He said as much to his producer Vivienne, who raised her eyebrows enigmatically.

'I didn't think she was your type.'

Jack laughed casually. 'Oh fuck no – I don't mean to go *there*.'

Vivienne, who had known him a long time, said, 'I wouldn't put it past you. What did you do to scare her off?'

'Ease up! I didn't do anything … yet.' He laughed. He liked being cheeky with Vivienne, whose shrewdness was a professional front. She was what people in the know called a Melbourne Art Woman and like every MAW she sported dyed, dramatic hair and chunky beads, which she fingered thoughtfully now.

'I was hoping she'd come out of her shell. But she seems to be … what's the right expression?'

'She's about as useful as a cock in a monastery,' said Jack.

'Really,' sighed Vivienne. 'One day you're going to get in trouble for saying things like that.'

'You think so? Hmm.' Jack pretended to consider it. 'Hey, I'm sure Hannah's lovely. Really, she's a sweet girl. I just find her fundamentally uninspiring.'

'You're such a dramatist. You'll be pleased to know her contract expires at the end of our season and she won't be coming on the regional tour.'

'You'd better make sure. It's not that I couldn't *tolerate* her … I just don't think she's a good fit.'

Just then he met Hannah's eye. She had been lurking in her usual pose just out of sight, party to their entire conversation. Her colour was high and she had that stricken look he'd come to recognise, but before he could stammer an apology, she turned and hurried off.

Twenty years later, her name popped up in his list of suggested friends. He clicked on the tile and was redirected to her profile, which showed a more mature and – he had to admit – rather gorgeous woman. Her hair was cut into a dangerous bombshell bob. In many of the photos she wore red lipstick, but now there was a wry self-assuredness in her pouty looks.

He spent longer than necessary trawling through her photos. When he was satisfied he had seen enough he clicked 'Add Friend', imagining what would happen once she accepted him, the conversation they would have. Once he'd warmed her up a little, he might even suggest they get a drink.

It became very important that she accept his friend request. Jack checked his account with a regularity verging on obsession, but two weeks later there was still no sign. More time passed and still his friend request hung pending. It bruised his ego, but he convinced himself that Hannah hadn't seen it. Then quite by chance he spotted her at the Woolies in Coburg, where he'd gone to get Elizabeth some rice.

Hannah was wearing a short plaid skirt and her hair was held back with a velvet headband, gratifyingly suggestive of a schoolgirl. At first he didn't recognise her – he simply thought, *That's what I like.* Then suddenly: *It's her!*

How clever of fate to throw them back together. He trailed her around the supermarket, looking for an opportunity to introduce himself. When she stopped before the bags of rice he thought it was his chance. But before he could approach her he was intercepted by a short, mannish woman whose earlobes had been stretched with large black discs the size of dollar coins. There was about the pair an air of satisfaction known to recent couples; he could tell by the involved and happy way they were discussing types of grain. Jack hung back, confronted with this new reality. The mannish one said something funny and Hannah threw her head back so her hair danced as she laughed.

'Are you right mate?'

The mannish one had noticed him.

'Sorry – yes – I'm just – there we go.' He flung a packet of rice into his basket, but not before there dawned in Hannah's eyes the light of recognition.

As he scurried off he overheard her saying to her partner, 'That old white guy – I knew him. He was such an arsehole.'

The women laughed. 'Men like that are—'

Shaken to his core, Jack drove back from Woolworths in a state of near hysteria. Navigating traffic, grappling with rare feelings of inadequacy. Looking at his hairline in the mirror – had it receded? Was it getting deeper, the furrow in his brow? He felt he had been wildly misrecognised. Jack, an old white guy? It simply didn't resonate. She had the wrong impression!

'Be honest Elizabeth,' he said when he got home. 'Do you think I'm old?'

Elizabeth paused and looked up from her laptop. 'Of course not. I mean, I don't think about it.'

'No, seriously. Do you think I'm like ... an *old white guy*?'

'Well, technically ...'

'You know what I mean!'

'Try not to take yourself too seriously,' she said, putting her arms around him. 'What's prompted this? Did you run into one of your old conquests in the supermarket?'

He disentangled himself. 'Here's your rice.'

'Brown rice ... Didn't I say to get Basmati?'

In the garden shed, where Elizabeth stored the remains of all her failed attempts at maintenance, he surreptitiously texted his ex-wife. *Do you ever feel like we're getting old?*

Diana did not reply.

Henceforth a plan took shape. He would seduce Hannah – he must. It wasn't anything he felt he needed to explain. He had no way of reaching her, but Jack trusted he would eventually run into her again.

AS IT HAPPENED, HE did not have long to wait. After the bad reviews, Jack's career had taken a little downturn and he wasn't sure what path to follow next. His superannuation was a sad state of affairs but he was too close to seventy to get a real job. Successive Liberal governments meant no funding for the arts and he had missed out on the few remaining grants. Then there was Weinstein, the public outings, the whole sleazy affair with Geoffrey Rush.

The fear in his circles was palpable. All the men he knew were acting very pious.

Even the usual pub talk was abandoned. Now when they caught up, Jack and his friends said things like, *Did you hear Candace Green got the MacPherson Fellowship?*

Candace Green? Well done Candace!

Yes, good on Candace, she deserves it!

Back in the day they would have reminded each other that Candace was a nightmare. Someone would have called her a diva or a bitch. The rumour that she sucked off Bill McAllister for a shot at the role of Lady Macbeth in his production (1997, critically acclaimed) might well have been bandied around. But now, once the initial congratulations were over, they sipped their beers and were grave.

Things had changed dramatically, and while Jack did not begrudge women their right to complain about real offences, he feared the hysteria was disproportionate to what had actually taken place. He was pierced with the realisation that he was never going to make it – that he was past the point of making it despite whatever success he had enjoyed. His last play's reception only cemented this awful truth. Disregarding who he was or what he knew about himself, he had become a stereotype. He had become an *old white man*.

He took care to show humility while panicking in private. Various thoughts crossed his mind. He could get a tiny little bit of botox, just to firm up his frown line. He could ask Elizabeth if she wanted to have a baby. He could try and collaborate with someone young, hot and diverse – he would even consent to being paid less so long as he was properly credited for the script. But no – that wouldn't do. He didn't like collaboration. He didn't want his vision circumscribed. He had been around too long to watch his Ps and Qs.

Then he landed on a brilliant idea. He would retreat into the shadowy world of academia, where things always stayed the same, to indulge a passion project: the thesis on Beckett he had often longed to write.

He chose an institution and formulated a proposal. Unbelievably, when perusing the list of potential supervisors, he landed on Hannah's profile. In this photo, like the other, her lips were bolded with a shock of red and there was no mistaking her despite the formal setting. And while her expression was subdued there was something inviting, Jack thought, in the way she leaned against her desk.

His pulse quickened. It seemed too perfect a coincidence to ignore, the deus ex machina to their play. So without pausing too long to examine his motives, he typed an email and clicked *send*.

THE FIRST TIME HE went to her office, she sat on one side of the desk and he sat on the other.

'So,' she said, leaning back and crossing her legs. 'Shall we address the elephant in the room?'

His mouth was dry but he played it cool. 'The...elephant?'

'I have to admit that when I received your email, I was a little taken back. I don't know if you remember me—'

'I remember,' Jack said quickly, eager to give the right impression. 'I've been wondering how to apologise for what happened ... I was such an arrogant bastard back then. You know how it is ... My work had a certain cachet.'

Hannah snorted. 'I'm sorry – yes – I suppose it did.'

Jack was suddenly offended. Her dismissiveness – the way she emphasised the past tense.

He retaliated. 'I assume that's why you chose to work with me.'

'Why I chose to work with you ... hmm. We're not here to talk about me. Let's talk about you.'

Jack was flustered. 'If you remember, your contract had expired.'

'I'm not interested in what you believe did or didn't happen. Let's stay on track – we haven't got much time.'

'Look, I think you have the wrong impression. I never dismissed you. Actually, I'm pretty sure I tried to convince Vivienne to let you stay.'

Hannah looked past him, out the window. The situation had gotten out of control and neither party seemed to know how to move on. When at last she spoke, she said, 'Would you mind if we took this elsewhere? It's stifling in this room.'

They walked across campus and then toward Lygon Street. It was the start of semester and the plane trees were just on the brink of losing their leaves; some flitted past them as they walked.

They sat down at a café. It was warm and many other couples dined out on the footpath. The street had an air of easy sociability, even flirtation. He wondered why she'd brought him here. It was not exactly the right way to establish professional boundaries.

'Shall we order drinks?' he asked, just as Hannah said, 'Sorry about this. I felt we needed a change of scenery.'

'No, no. It makes sense. I'm sorry our history has been ... fraught.'

'Yes,' she said. 'And no, I don't think I'll drink. I have to work after this.'

Again, the way she said it irritated him. Her comment was designed to establish dominance – anyone could see that. Rage surged through him and he let it push aside his feelings of inadequacy. He had genuinely wanted to make amends, but now he imagined wrenching her arm and pinning her against a wall to kiss her forcefully, like a man in the movies.

'No worries,' he said. 'I hope you don't mind if I order something.'

'Go ahead.'

They studied their menus in silence. When it was time to order, Jack went up to the counter and asked for two negronis and a bottle of their second-cheapest white, telling the waiter not to bring out their food until both the aperitifs and bottle had been drunk. It was an act of deception that surprised even himself, but he sensed that Hannah was playing with him and he was determined to regain the upper hand. He would get her drunk, he decided. Then they would see if she didn't warm to him.

Back at the table Hannah looked surprised, but seeing Jack's determination seemed to resign herself to being sportive. It was as if she said, *alright – have it your way*. Wearily, she drew the negroni toward herself across the table.

'You guessed my favourite drink,' she said.

So she'd begrudge him that. Jack smiled, feeling like he'd won a point. 'Now do you believe me when I say I have my talents?'

Despite herself, amusement flickered on her face. She sat back and sipped.

'I didn't mean to be too personal before,' she began. 'Believe me, that's all in the past. In fact, my failure with you and Vivienne led me to Goldilocks, which as you know is an all-woman company, where I was determined to prove myself and was eventually made associate producer. In a way, that wouldn't have happened without you. So thanks.'

She clinked his class.

'Cheers,' he said.

Things appeared to be turning round. Their food came out and steamed between them. Jack was chatty, voluble with the wine. Hannah smiled at appropriate times and he allowed himself to picture what it would be like to have her in bed. He had been distracted by his pride, but now he was determined to be charming. He refilled his wine. Hannah hadn't touched her glass. They finished their meal and then their plates were cleared away.

'Well,' said Hannah. 'That's about the end of my lunch break. I should get back.'

'This has been nice,' said Jack. 'Really lovely.' He fought the urge to reach for her hand, settling instead on a look which conveyed his desire, or so he thought, in a completely non-threatening way. 'We should do this again.'

'No, I don't think so,' she said firmly. 'You must know this sort of thing doesn't happen all the time.'

'Okay. Right. I wasn't trying to suggest—'

'Suggestions aside, I am here to supervise your thesis. I agreed because I'm fascinated by your proposal – you said you want to interrogate the resonances between Beckett's Theatre of the Absurd and current breakdowns in political speech. If that's true, I want to work with you. I want us to work together.'

'So do I,' he stammered, knowing he had been caught out.

'Good,' she said. 'See you next time, at my office.' Her full glass of wine sat on the table, untouched. 'You have that – I already said I didn't want it.'

Humiliated, Jack paid the bill and left. It was far more than he could afford. At home that afternoon, he continued getting drunk. He smoked a spliff and let his feelings of dejection and frustration morph into full-blown paranoia. Hannah thought he was pathetic, Hannah thought he was an idiot, old, an ageing lothario. Hannah was herself an arrogant bitch and also, most likely, frigid.

In the morning he woke to several missed calls from Elizabeth and one from his daughter Liv. He pushed his phone aside and drank some water. In the unforgiving light of morning, it was clear that not only had his seduction failed, but his behaviour at lunch was completely unacceptable. The realisation crushed him. He had been so sure of his plan to seduce her. But it seemed those days were over – how had he not noticed?

Feeling contrite, Jack threw himself into his research. By the time his confirmation came around, he and Hannah had struck upon a tentative peace. Over the next year, it hesitatingly developed into sympathy. He remembered a time when it was possible to be excited by your own ideas, such as he had been in the early days of his career, working on devised theatre with a bunch of artists, actors and eccentrics. Forgetting his singular desire to possess her, Jack decided he liked working with her instead.

But every so often she'd withdraw her favour, and he would perceive something chilly and unknowable in Hannah, something he longed to master. Always, then, the fervour came upon him – changed in nature, though just as strong as before.

ACT III

Jack's favourite part of writing plays is the preliminary read-through. He likes sitting with the actors in a circle, listening as they stumble through his script. Only then, while the play exists as both text and performance, as both more and less than he imagined, does he sense the intense potential of dramatic art.

He has always been attracted to ideas in the subjunctive. The women he pursues, the books he hasn't read, future projects, burgeoning themes. In reality, he is often disappointed. By now, he is drunk. The bottle stands empty on the table. He longs to speak with someone, but there is no one he can reach. Somewhere in the house, that door is still banging. He drinks his wine and smokes and ruminates.

In the bathroom, he stares into the mirror. His eyes are bloodshot and his silver hair and face have taken on a scary pallor. The man he sees is hardly recognisable. Around nine, the wind dies down and leaves the whole place still. Jack rolls himself a spliff and smokes it on the verandah, craving lightness, but the drug makes him uneasy and compounds his loneliness.

Just three months ago, he was in Paris. He was on his own then too, although it never crossed his mind to be lonely. Some French theorists from Université PSL were putting on a Beckett Symposium and Hannah had helped him secure funding to attend. She even insisted that he stay in her late father's apartment, which had been vacant since his death.

When he arrived in June, it was warm and the Seine was flat and green like a paint swatch. Jack had been to Paris in the 1980s and besides some cosmetic details he found the city had not changed; Europe, he thought, was reassuringly settled in its ways.

The apartment was large and cluttered with her father's things. Feeling slightly pervy, Jack studied the framed

pictures, records and CDs, some jackets in the wardrobe
and a shelf full of books. He was pleased to see many that
he liked. It was the same with the music collection – Talking Heads, Brian Eno, Chick Corea, Billie Holiday – all the
artists he admired. He remembered something Hannah said
about her father. 'You're actually quite similar. How old are
you? You're probably about the same age. I think he would
have liked you. You remind me of him, sometimes.'

It was a weird thing to say and now it seemed quite
pointed, suggesting she wanted something from Jack that
he had always longed to give her. Platonic love or an Electra
complex – it was stirring either way.

Buoyed by this supposition, his fortnight in Paris
passed in a haze of summer light, optimism and very good
wine. On the last night of the symposium he got drunk
with some people he had met and walked home in the rain.
Back at the apartment, his gaze fell unsteadily upon a large,
heavy book splayed seductively between the bookcase and
the desk. It was a lovely object, a massive hardback tome
with creamy, deckled edges. Retrieving it from where it lay,
he saw it was an anthology of critical writings on Beckett.

Again he was struck by a sense of strange plotting.
Leafing through, he discovered a section devoted to some
grainy black and white photographs of Beckett's earliest
productions, including spectacular shots of the premiere
of *Waiting for Godot* at the Théâtre de Babylone in Paris
in the winter of 1953. Studying the photos, Jack noticed
something wedged against the spine. At first he thought it

was attached, but when he cracked it open further, a polaroid fell into his lap. It was a picture of someone's feet. He tingled. It felt as it had when, aged eleven, he followed Graham down to the foreshore and watched him fuck a girl beneath the pier. He had sensed that Graham knew that he was there and still he loitered, breathless with wrongdoing.

The feet were pale and slender, elegant, but the toes were short and stubby with broad, hard-looking nails. The combination of those ugly toes with such an intelligent foot was incredibly sensuous. It suggested something dark and cryptic about their owner; some clever, hidden quick.

Bewildered, Jack shoved the polaroid back inside the book and slammed it shut. A minute or so elapsed and then, feeling bolder, he fished it out again. His mind went back to all those years ago when Hannah wore red lipstick to opening night; how it had looked so slutty on her pure, anxious face. He realised this was what he meant when he said, 'It suits you,' and why she must have run to the toilets and taken it off. He had thought, back then, that he had frightened her. But with the picture in his hands he saw, quite suddenly, that she was frightened of herself.

A WAVE OF NAUSEA overcomes him and he retches off the verandah. Once he is finished, he rinses out his mouth with wine. He knows he should drink some water and lie down, but instead he finishes the spliff in two long drags. His head spins and spins, but this time he doesn't spew.

Returning to the bedroom, Jack rifles around in his bag, tossing clothes and shaving gear aside until he finds the book he carried home from Paris. Technically he stole it, although there is no one to berate him for it now. He opens the book at the fingered page, cracking it all the way down to the binding. There is the polaroid, just as it had been when he first found it.

He takes it out and holds it in his lap. Emotion leaps into his throat, but he cannot distinguish whether it is grief or lust, regret or rage. He thinks of his final day in Paris, how he went to the Louvre, leaving the polaroid in its book beside the bed. He had felt confused and out of sorts, his mind racing. Were they Hannah's feet and did she mean to leave it there, and was he meant to see it? In the museum, the crowds were oppressive. He locked himself inside a toilet stall, sat on the seat and tried to clear his head.

An email from the coordinator of his graduate program popped up on his phone, marked urgent. It did not say how Hannah died – only that it had been unexpected. He read the email twice and then deleted it, convinced that it was a mistake. Then he washed his hands, left the toilets and wandered through the galleries, looking at the treasures of his culture for a while.

Even now, he does not know many of the details. He does not know who to ask. He does not know where he stands and feels himself to be in limbo, worried that he has no right to mourn her. Who is he, in the end, but her student? And who was she, ultimately, but the woman assigned to supervise his PhD?

How many times in the intervening months has he asked himself these questions?

Desperately, he reaches for the bottle, knocking it to the ground. It rolls and bounces, the wine spreading in a violent, bloody stain across the carpet. He swears and pelts it against the wall.

Feeling reckless, he rolls and starts to smoke another joint until his limbs are jelly and his tongue is large and livid in his mouth. He has an urge to remove his shirt and jumper, which he does, throwing them over the door. He opens the Beckett book and finds the polaroid. Hannah's feet are as he left them: mysterious and slightly obscene. Sitting on the bed, he takes his cock out of his pants and strokes the head and shaft until he's hard. Placing the polaroid where he can see it, Jack pumps his cock – slowly at first, then faster and faster and with mounting fury, faster and faster and faster until he suddenly comes and with a ragged moan that's closer to a sob he shudders, curling into himself, feeling all the uncertainty and grief he has been holding explode richly over his hands and belly, and as the semen starts to cool he stays there gripping his wet deflating cock and moaning, listening to the long, unbearable cries of a wounded animal emitting from his mouth, cries which waver and then pale, and eventually die out.

Then he jams the polaroid against the spine and snaps the creamy pages shut.

ACT IV

Towelling off, Jack feels like a monster. He feels worse than he has ever felt. He is a sick old man – yes – a sick, lonely old perv rattling around this haunted house writing himself off and wanking over failed conquests. The door is still banging and its ceaseless rhythm jangles his nerves. Possessed by a recklessness bred of self-loathing, he smokes the rest of the joint.

The paranoia sets in for good when he's in bed, willing himself to sleep, and it is not long before he reaches a state of pure terror. Every few minutes, he raises his head from the pillow to listen for ghosts. The wind, starting up again, is a waif begging to be let inside. The sensor light turns on and off, and footsteps cross the porch. The clothes he flung over the door become a figure which then squats atop his chest, an incubus about to choke or penetrate him mercilessly, before inserting one of its long fingers up his nose.

A single flash of lightning illuminates the bedroom and is gone.

A shock of rain lands on the roof.

The house begins to shake.

Crockery leaps from the shelves. The waif resumes her scratching at the window and the cottage's foundations start to groan like something ancient waking from its sleep. In the hallway, the credenza disgorges books and ornaments, its broken shells. The child's creepy painting dances from its hook above the table like a poltergeist and flies on owlish wings across the room. Jack hears voices. He hears things shattering. He shakes violently, clutching the doona around his vulnerable, naked body, which feels in this moment like the body of a child. Reaching his edge, he passes out.

The shaking stops. Returning to consciousness, he recovers his will enough to disengage from the foetal position and leap out of the bed. He dresses quickly and begins to run around the house gathering up his things, shoving books and food and toiletries into bags and sprinting out to the car, looking over his shoulder the whole time. He curses the lack of reception and thinks that if he's murdered or possessed, no one will ever find him. Insensible with fear he jumps into the driver's seat, shoves the Suby into gear and fangs it back to the road.

But the ordeal is not quite over. As the wine, dope and adrenaline compete in his system he speeds through Portsea and Sorrento, where everyone has gone to bed. He feels like the last man on earth in Blairgowrie, passing eerie shopfronts and parked cars. In Rye the rain hits, burying his windscreen underneath a sheet of silver. He aquaplanes just as a cop car pulls out from a side street, tailing him for a kilometre before disappearing down another road. In his terror he pictures losing control of the car and crashing into the bay. He begins composing frantic messages to his loved ones – Diana and their daughters, Elizabeth, even Graham. He drives recklessly for he doesn't know how long.

It is not until Jack reaches the city fringe that he switches on the radio and takes a few deep breaths. There has been an earthquake. Not a big one – only 2.7 on the Richter scale. He pulls into the emergency lane, stills the Suby's engine, finds his phone and calls Elizabeth.

ACT V

She picks up on the first ring. He can hear a party in the background and the sounds of music, talking, tinkling glasses.

'What time is it? Are you okay?'

'Elizabeth – oh my god.'

'There's been an earthquake!' she exclaims. 'Some glasses smashed and now we're all excited. Did you feel it?'

'I'm sitting on the side of the freeway. Where are you?'

'What, why? I'm at a party, remember – Martina is leaving JLM. I can't hear you … hold on while I go outside.'

A truck passes and its headlights sweep the car. Jack is reminded of the single flash of lightning, his terror at the cottage, what he did with Hannah's photo. He can't believe that he – who does not believe in ghosts, except as a theatrical device – failed to recognise the earthquake as a natural phenomenon and convinced himself that he was being haunted. There is a hollow feeling in the pit of his stomach which he understands is shame.

'Okay, wow, it's cold out here … Jack, are you crying?'

'Liz, I want to explain … Something happened when I was in Paris. I didn't want to tell you because of … I don't know. Tonight when the earthquake struck I freaked out and got in my car and left. I don't think I can go back there. I feel completely fucked.'

There is silence on the other end of the phone. On the radio, the hosts are wondering whether earthquakes have anything to do with climate change. They play a song he doesn't recognise as the narrow crescent of the moon struggles to emerge from racing clouds. Then Elizabeth says, 'I know about Hannah, Jack. I read it in the email. It's alright … no one will hold it against you. You're grappling with a loss. People will understand. I'm leaving soon. Come over to mine.'

He drives slowly. From the freeway it's an easy drive to Coburg, where he parks outside Elizabeth's house. Nothing seems amiss or out of place, as if the earthquake never reached this side of town, and Jack has the strange sense of returning from a distant country full of new ideas to find that nothing, in his absence, has changed.

He lets himself in with the spare key, unsurprised to find himself clutching the heavy, hardback book. Elizabeth is not yet home from her party, but Jack is comforted by her smell as he pulls the covers back and settles in between her sheets. Before relaxing fully, he turns on the bedside lamp and parts the book in the photographic section, but even as his fingers search the spine he knows the polaroid is gone.

A long exhale tumbles from his lips. He closes his eyes, letting his head fall back against the pillow. Somewhere in the house a door opens and clicks shut; Elizabeth is home, turning on lights, taps, taking off her make-up, opening the fridge. He listens to her treading softly round the house, feeling emptied of everything, finally, as though he has been exorcised.

She opens the door so that a crack of light falls gently on his face. 'Are you still awake?'

'I feel so strange. Clean and bare and empty, like you could see right through me to the other side.'

Elizabeth giggles drunkenly. 'That reminds me. Grace came home from school and told her first joke today. She said, *Why was the ghost so bad at faking it?*'

'I went beyond. It was … Why?' he mumbles, meeting the edge of sleep.

'*Because he was transparent!* Jack – are you still with me? Isn't that clever … Jack?'

FARROW

ARLIER, THE GARDENER HAD woken to a break
in the weather, the pale sun struggling through. He
had fed the dog, made coffee, got on his jacket and
boots and gone outside to work. He did not intuit
anything or have a special feeling; it was merely a case of
getting something done as long as the rain held off.

All morning he worked hard restoring order, for the
summer had been unusually wet and now his garden
dripped with foliage that was altogether rampant. It had
always been abundant – since moving here he'd grown
things without effort, even the okra and avocadoes he had
struggled with in other places. But the wet had made it wild.
Thuggish blackberries and nettles crowded out the veggies.
Errant herbs self-seeded in the cracks. The slugs were growing fat and shiny and the soil was dark and moist.

It became hot and steamy in the garden. Convinced of
itself, the sun shone fully on the rain-jewelled leaves and

everything was freshly bright and urgent. The gardener settled into his work and felt like he was making progress. Things were getting neater. By midday, he had cleared a decent patch of weeds and dumped them in the compost. It was overflowing, emanating a thick, distracting smell.

His phone rang. 'Hello?'

'It's time now,' his uncle said simply. 'The doctors said it's time.'

The gardener rested on his heels for a moment to recover. Damp earth stained his pants at the knees and he felt the chill of it wind through him. 'I can't believe it,' he said.

'I know. Tough old bird. Do you think you'll make it out to see her?'

'I'm in the garden,' he said. It wasn't really an answer, but he was having trouble concentrating because of the smell coming from the compost. The word he thought of was *fecund*. It didn't match what he was hearing. It didn't match what he knew of death, or the sterile room in which his grandma laboured, or her ragged breathing punctuated by the hum and beep of hospital machines. It didn't match anything. It bordered on obscene.

His grandmother was the only parent he had really known, and the gardener did not know how he'd feel once she was gone. There was a hardness in her, he thought, which had always made it seem like she would live forever.

'You know she never once said she loved me,' he said, before he knew what he was saying.

'I know,' said his uncle. 'I know what she was like.'

WHEN HIS GRANDMOTHER ARRIVED from Ireland, she
suffered for want of green. She had no people either here
or there and everywhere she went the colours of the landscape struck her as unfeeling. To her surprise she missed
the dense, wet closeness of her home, even though she
knew that home had a tiresome way of holding people and
resented its embrace.

A year passed. In Melbourne she found work at an
Anglican girls' school, where her accent made her feel
like an outsider and she didn't tell them she was Catho-
lic. Although she'd done it back in Ireland she did not like
teaching, for she had a hatred of banality and no natural
ease with children. It had always been her dream to study
medicine, having seen, as a girl, the body of the neighbour
McKinnon laid out in the house next door.

It had made an impression – the two lit candles at the
bedhead, the curtains drawn and mirrors covered and the
man's huge, heavy face. 'Are ye frightened at all?' her mother
had asked – but no, she was not frightened. She had looked
upon the dead man wondering what it would be like to
unbutton his waistcoat, his shirt and then his skin to look
inside. In her heart of hearts she knew she would have made
a fine doctor, but it was not so easy for a woman of her time.

After about a year she accepted a position at a rural
school north-west of Melbourne. The town was small
and unfamiliar and the people were unfriendly. Running
through it was a river which looked innocent enough but
seemed to rise without the slightest warning at the mere

mention of rain. That winter, there were floods. The town was thrown into a state of emergency and in the excitement she agreed to marry a local farmer's son.

It wasn't the worst thing that could have happened. It got her out of teaching, and she figured that if she wasn't going back to Ireland she might as well put down her roots. Her husband was a soft touch and she reckoned he'd allow her certain freedoms; he would tolerate her longing to engage her hands and mind with something more than folding sheets. They were married at St. Patrick's in December, she with her bouquet of yellow roses, delphiniums and hydrangeas and just three people on her side.

Their wedding night was spent in town and then she joined her husband on his parents' farm. The Waters were hard people who had been in town since it was settled. They extracted what they could from the land and only mixed with other families who had been around as long as they had. In the first months of her marriage she would often walk the boundary, wondering about the names of things.

'What is this one called?' she asked her husband, spreading her hands over the rough hide of a tree, where rivulets were carved as though by many streams.

'Maybe some kind of box,' he said. 'All I know is that it burns hot and long and clean.'

'And these?' she asked of flowers, the petals white and pink and waxy.

Her husband looked at her strangely. 'Why do you care, anyway? You won't find anyone round here who bothers much with flowers; our time is taken up with more important things.'

So she stopped asking questions and learned to treat the land as criminal, a wayward force that needed to be disciplined. They cut down trees, ploughed paddocks and sprayed weeds. Her husband showed her how to ride the four-wheeler, drive the tractor and put the feed out for the cows. He showed her how to turn the sod, plant seeds and grow crops of canola, lucerne and wheat. He showed her how to slash the blackberries and nettles which grew thick along the driveway, and with all these things to do she had no time to walk the boundary; her days were full of more important things.

When the two old Waters died, the farm was left to them. She and her husband kept the dairy cows and later she convinced him to invest in pigs. Their short gestation meant a high return on their investment. If she could make them farrow twice a year, with ten to fifteen pigs per litter, that meant having money left over at the end of each month. When she suggested it, her husband looked at her like she'd been given him by God.

'We'll be rolling in it if your scheme comes off,' he marvelled.

'Let's not count our chickens before they're hatched. The hard times are with us yet.'

'You always know what's best. That's why I married you.'

'That's why you married me,' she echoed, though her husband's adoration had begun to grate on her. She took on more responsibilities: helping with the farm work, balancing the accounts and keeping house. By the time her duties were over for the day, her husband had long gone to bed. In the morning she rose early, before it was light, and went out to the animals. She discovered her own skill attending to the ones that were sick or new or labouring, especially the bellowing sows whose births she'd oversee. It was not quite medicine, but it was something. The farrowing went beautifully. Just as she had promised, she coaxed her sows to give birth twice a year, and by Christmas they had more piglets than they knew what to do with.

'You have the gift of fertility!' her husband beamed, surveying the farrowing crates. 'My very own Ceres!'

'Enough, away with you. 'Tis only in their nature.'

Her husband took her by the hand. 'You'll make a wonderful mother,' he sighed wistfully and smiled.

But her pregnancies exhausted her and made her sick. She bore a girl and then a boy and decided enough was enough. Even as they grew, her children disappointed her. There wasn't any reason. Her husband tried to compensate by playing cards with them and taking them out fishing, answering their painful questions, buying them milkshakes and driving places on a Sunday. He longed for a large, boisterous family but every time he pestered her to have another baby her response was just the same.

'Breeding is for animals,' she would say. 'We had better leave it up to them.'

When her husband died of heart failure at the age of fifty-five, she felt herself exhale for the first time since they married. She was a widow before she went through menopause, but even though she had been left with grief and debt and running the farm she had also been given her livelihood. Finally master of herself she swore not to remarry, and what's more, to never give her love again.

She cut her hair and wore the same blue tracksuit every day. When it rained she swore, and when it was dry she swore again. Attending to the animals slowly lost its magic. She cursed the cost of feed, the weather, the bank, her daughter, the neighbours, politics, the times, becoming hardened like the family she married into. By the time the gardener came to live with her, his grandmother's heart was flinty. She had become ... what? Not harsh, exactly – caring in her way. She raised him the same as she raised her pigs and cows and cattle dogs: looking after them, making sure they were fed and housed and given purpose. She was not affectionate. She had lost her feeling for it, even if there was enough to go around.

Now she was dying at a nursing home in Clayton, the farm sold to move her into residential care. His grandmother was dying ... he tried to let this fact sink in. His grandmother – the woman who took care of him when his mother fell in love with an American named Mark, moved there and started a new family. The woman who raised him when his disconsolate father couldn't cope. Who once revealed that when she first received him, he unnerved her.

'Such a strange child,' she had said. 'Away with the fairies, always covered in dirt.'

He looked down at his hands, which were muddy from gardening, and fought a wave of nausea. It was true he had been dirty, and had suffered from a dearth of love. His grandmother's farm had been a place of exile, and although he came to love the shuffling wombats and the herds of kangaroos, the Friesians roaring at the fence when it was time for milking, the blackwood and the box, the sudden floods when water burst the levee he was haunted by abandonment, the ease with which his parents gave him up.

He had not been back since it was sold but now the memories rose in quick succession: the farmhouse sinking on its timber struts, lace curtains stained with age and cooking, the yard hen-pecked and muddy, his grandmother's hydrangeas changing colour based on ions in the soil. He was fascinated by these flowers, their clouds of tiny petals which would morph from blue to pink to white according to no reason he could see. It seemed mysterious, and when he asked her how she made her flowers change she winked and said it was a secret.

'Magic. If I told you I would have to kill you.'

He believed her. He had seen her bring a stillborn calf to life by pouring water in its ear. She could make things grow by simply willing it and he was conscious, too, that she could take all this away. For there had been a day when he had followed her to the farrowing crates and learned what she did to her piglets, the ones she didn't want. Even now, he shuddered to recall the way she cracked their baby skulls against the slate, the sound so routine and efficient, *thwack … thwack …* but muffled, like being stuck inside a jumper you'd been struggling to take off.

'It's more humane this way,' she snapped. 'Otherwise the little ones'll be crushed or eaten by their mothers.' She placed a hand on his cheek, a rare gesture of affection. Her tone softened. 'You'll understand some day. Nature has no kindness for the weak.'

Her logic made a brutal kind of sense, although the gardener always felt that it betrayed a lack of love. His childhood lacked intimacy. But then sometimes a sharp, unseasonable frost would freeze the water in the dog bowls, and there would be the wonder when he rushed outside first thing to crack it like a crème brûlée.

Which is to say, he thought of the farm, then and always, with mixed feelings.

And then there was the thing he dared not remember, the thing which reared up in him now. For he was often lonely at the farm, the only child for miles around, and lacking interaction he developed strange habits and ways of passing time, including a fascination for dirt.

THE GARDENER PUT HIS phone in his pocket. Urged by the memory, he leaned forward and pressed his hands into the soil. He leaned in close, recalling the strong desire to have some in his mouth. Not to eat, exactly, but to see how it would taste and feel.

Black soil tempted him back then, as did red and yellow clay. He preferred dense, compact types which he could hold without them breaking down, although he also loved to feel the soil getting slack as his saliva rushed into his mouth. He liked it when the dirt he held would smell like minerals and shit and sometimes he would shiver with an ancient pleasure when he sensed himself connecting to the leaves and bones and flesh which centuries of life had left behind. The best dirt was found around the compost heap, where the earth was rich and life sprung from decay. There was a kind of magic in its mysteries. Its aliveness while appearing to be sleeping. Its quickness while appearing to be dense.

At first he was young enough that his dirt-longing did not warrant much interrogation. He was simply following an instinct, paying attention to the world. Sweeping back the topsoil to expose the dark, wet layer beneath, everything felt suddenly more attuned; he moved in congruence with the earth's deep sighs and transports. The minute he put the dirt inside his mouth a great peace would overcome him, as though in containing the earth, he somehow felt contained.

This was reassuring in a time of neglect, for his grandmother refused to acknowledge the circumstances in which he'd come to live with her – refused even to mention, after she went to America, her daughter's name.

But as the gardener grew into puberty, his relation to his appetite became confused. Sex was another subject on which his grandmother was reticent, and being ill-informed about desire, his dirt-longing got all muddled up with nascent sexual knowledge. He began to suspect it was wrong, although thinking it perverse had no effect on his restraint; the more he tried denying it, the stronger his lust became.

He learned to be secret and even devious, figuring out ways to indulge his dirt-longing in secret. One memory pierced him now, of a period in which he was compelled to undress, apply mud to his entire body and wear it home beneath his clothes. The triumph was in covering himself completely, so that even while appearing clean he could smell and feel the mud all over him. He imagined it like a force field, protecting him from all the questions he did not know how to answer. But his grandmother had a keen sense of intuition. It upset him still to think of how she made him strip off in the kitchen, her cold efficiency, her ugly tone. How she quickly bundled up his clothes and took them to the laundry, how she made him stand there on the lino as she scrubbed him roughly with a face washer, every inch of him despite his being much too old. Her unbearable scrutiny. The cold, his shame, the lemon-scented soap. How she called him dirty – *a disgusting, dirty boy.*

After that, he tried to tamp his longing down. He discovered normal pleasures – masturbation, reading, video games – and gradually replaced his desire for dirt with desire for these other things. He made friends with some boys from town with whom he'd ride bikes and make prank calls; later, they would get drunk in paddocks and listen to 50 Cent. His grandmother was still watchful, but his behaviour convinced her he had gotten over his odd phase. It was a relief to them both. Growing up meant getting away from the ground – things had to become hygienic.

But oh – he felt it coursing through him now, after all these years lying dormant! Today should be a day of mourning, he thought, ashamed that it had loosed in him a strong desire to be free.

Dirty boy, he heard his grandmother say.

There came again the smell of compost. His grandmother once said that if she had her time again she never would have married, would never have had children, should not have settled on the farm. 'I only did what was expected,' she said. 'I thought I had no other choice.'

With these words racing through his blood he rose and walked toward the compost. There were the weeds he'd pulled this morning, mixed with kitchen scraps. There were the beetles and the fruit flies, whirring as he approached. Up close the smell was sensational, eye watering; he blinked back tears. Saliva rushed into his mouth, the kind which usually meant that he would vomit, except that now he felt ecstatic. His heart, he noticed, was beating very fast.

With strong, broad strokes he swept aside the surface layers of the compost to reveal what lay beneath. Steam rose up and when it dissipated, the gardener saw a dark cacophony of life. Everything was spoiled, but this spoiling, oh, how awesome! Again that word, *fecund,* a word he'd been avoiding because he thought he didn't have a choice.

Now it was all before him.

The tea-stained sludge glacially moving. The worms devotedly churning. The flies haphazardly scattering. The eggshells artfully breaking. The lemons slyly oozing. The tomatoes softly slumping. The foundered seedlings failing. The nasty nettles lingering. The weeds expiring bravely. The wizened flowers wasting. The putrid petals mouldering. The radish serenely sinking. The beetroot pinkly staining other scraps. The eye of a crinkled old potato opening and closing – winking, if you like. The slugs going cross-country. The enzymes working thanklessly. The thuggish blackberries with their vinegary drupelets, plunging deep or climbing high to spill their last seeds on the mound.

And – why not – the seasons ever changing.

Yes – the turning of the sphere. The deaths both small and little, unexpected and observed. The banalities in extremity, the uncommon days of mourning, the animals to slaughter, skull-crack against the slate. And elsewhere in the future, as much as in the past, the cervixes dilating and the babies sliding out. The journeys and abandonments, the children growing painfully, the summer wet, the river floods, the soil getting slack. The waste all decomposing, the spoiling made extraordinary, the shame and the humiliation mingling with the lemon smell. The loneliness, the rages, the passions he'd forgotten; how they lived inside him, how they lived beneath the soil.

The soil! The gardener dropped to his knees beside the compost heap and started digging. The ground was soft and wet and gave in easily. He made a hole the size of his hand

and then the size of his knee. Soon, or so it felt to him, he had excavated a space roughly the size of himself. As he lay down, the ground received him openly. It transported him. That's how he felt – transported to a place he'd always longed to be.

Tears ran down his face and wet the soil. The gardener felt strangely porous, as if the earth's deep energy were running through him. He closed his eyes and thought of his grandmother, her unease with children, her hardness and her constancy, her longing and regret. She had let the life in her go stale. Opening his eyes, he sat up slowly.

He scooped some dirt. Then, he opened his mouth.

KINSHIP

TONIGHT MARTY IS AT the lodge, the collar of their good shirt chafing their neck, which is hot and raw with the day's burn. At their back the lodge is lit up like a cruise ship and sounds of revelry echo through the night. Beyond the verandah, the bristling lawn rolls down to a jetty reaching out into the inky lake. A pelican cruises by, the wind in its feathers. Marty thinks of their mother's hands.

It is New Year's Eve, just a few minutes to twelve. Soon the clock will tick over and the world will be renewed, their failings erased, the past year altered, retroactively, by the force of good intentions. Marty has been longing for this year to be over, but now, standing in the dark on the empty verandah, they feel mournful at its passing.

Inside, Hinemoana is arguing with Marty's brother Larry. The three of them have come on holiday together, leaving Marty's mother fretful and confused at a nursing home in Melbourne. The trip was meant to give them all a break, but since they arrived in this town by the lake each day has been full of estrangement.

Over the past few months Marty and Larry have watched their young, fantastic mother's memory fall away like wet sand. They have bickered, snapped and cried in each other's arms. It is tiring, all this holding. Holding each other. Holding their mother. Holding down their jobs. Holding it together. Holding up.

Their mother is not old. At the age of fifty-nine she was diagnosed with younger onset dementia; three months later they got her on the pension and into residential care. Another month, another unsuccessful round of IVF for Marty and Hen, more grief, more dollars down the drain. When people ask how they are going Marty says, 'You know how it is. When it rains, it pours.' It's so stupid. What else is there to say?

Bad things come in threes. It's superstitious, but Marty has been wondering what the hell will happen next. Time is running out. They do not wish to carry this run of bad luck into tomorrow, lest it taint the promise of a brand-new year.

Now Marty can hear Hen and Larry talking, their frantic whispers getting audible as their argument heats up.

'Don't you dare say anything, Larry!'

'What did I say? What?'

'I told you I'll talk to them!'

'I'm just saying, soon it will be pretty fucking obvious.'

'Shut the fuck up, Larry. For fuck's sake.'

Marty drifts away from the lodge and looks across the water. It's a dark night, the moon obscured by heavy cloud. They cannot tell where the lake ends and the shore begins but they can hear the water lapping gently at the jetty's pylons. The sound is eerily disembodied. Marty feels adrift, apart from things. They wish they were back in Melbourne, getting stoned in their own backyard, sounds of other parties drifting over from the neighbours' houses. This place is too remote, too silent and too wild.

Just then, Marty feels Hinemoana at their side. 'The countdown's starting in a second,' she says.

'Oh,' says Marty. 'Do you need me?'

'Who else am I going to kiss at midnight?' Hen smiles. 'Come on Marty. Come inside.'

THEY LEFT MELBOURNE EARLIER that week. The drive was boring: one long straight line through farmland, flooded paddocks, town after shitty Gippsland town. It was Larry's idea to come back to Mallacoota, where they holidayed once as kids. Back then their mum had a friend with a mudbrick flat and for a while she had a boyfriend, Tommy, who taught them how to fish.

'Tommy! Now he was a great guy. I'd have to say he was my favourite of all of Mum's boyfriends. Do you remember why they broke up?' asked Larry in the car.

'Oh, probably the usual. Mum got bored or we needed a new place to live.'

'Come on. It wasn't always like that.'

'What? I'm just saying she had a pattern.'

'Anyway, this guy Tommy—Hen, are you listening? This guy Tommy once caught ten fish with ... wait for it ... a fucking ciggie butt!'

'No ...' said Hen in disbelief.

'Serious,' said Larry. 'He was out in the boat one day and hadn't planned on fishing, but for some reason – intuition or whatever – he was taken by the mood to catch a fish. There was a rod in the boat but no bait, so he used the cigarette he'd been smoking. Sure enough, soon as he dropped a line he got a bite! And then he used that fish to catch all the others.' Larry sighed. 'Ahh. I love that story.'

'I didn't know you were so nostalgic,' said Marty.

'Course you did! He's a big softie, aren't you Laz,' said Henny.

'I'm a sensitive guy,' said Larry. 'What can I say?'

Lately, Larry has been spending a lot of time at their house. It's nice, actually, like when they lived together in the past. Marty likes getting home after a shitty day at work or a frustrating session with their mother at the nursing home, walking out the back and finding Larry skinning up and playing records. He usually hands Marty a beer and then Henny will appear, looking radiant, her long hair dripping as if she'd been for a swim or something, but it's only 'cause she's had a shower. Then the three of them sit and talk about books and records, work, people they know. They rarely speak about their mother. Lately, this was just what Marty needed.

'Anyway,' said Larry, 'what's wrong with a bit of nostalgia?'

'If you're not careful it will kill you.'

'I wouldn't go that far,' said Hen. 'Maybe it will just make you depressed.'

'That's it then – say no to nostalgia. To the future! To progress! To infinity and beyond!' Larry put his foot on the accelerator and the car shot up the back of the one in front.

Marty rammed their foot against the floor instinctively. 'Laz!'

'I'm not even close! Relax. You need a drink.'

'Guys,' said Hen, de-escalating. 'We're on holiday. Let's get excited. Let's just say, right now, that we're going to have a good time.'

'That's right,' said Larry. 'You've gotta stop being so pessimistic Marty. Have faith.'

And then Henny sang, 'Faith-a-faith-a-faith-a!'

'Alright alright. We're having a good time.'

'That's what we like! Now, we hear the fish are biting Marty, do we not?'

It's true they'd heard the lake was full of flathead. In the old days, thought Marty, serious fishermen would have used an almanac. Flathead, especially the big predacious Duskies, were sensitive to the pull of the moon. The best time to catch a flathead was on a runout tide, three days before the full.

Marty made a quick calculation: that would make it New Year's Eve. It seemed auspicious. But as they drove into town and saw how everything had changed, not just with passing years but since those massive fires, all those spindly calcined eucalypts now sporting epicormic fluff like feather boas, and the lake stained black from all the tannins, Marty did feel nostalgic for the past.

For Betka Beach. For picnics at Goanna Bay, big lizards hulking up to steal their sausages from the grill. For someone's dinghy, which they took out on the lake. For people playing music around a fire. For Tommy as he showed them how to bait a line, clamping the smelly prawn between two fingers, placing his can of beer to the side. Their mother's friend Kelly singing that one Bob Marley song. Shells, books, board games, sinkers. Hooking Larry in the lip one time when Marty went to cast, tugging forward and hearing his funny yelp. Skipjack, whiting, bream. Marty's first obsession with flathead. How Tommy once caught a big one which they ate with chips their mother cooked in a coal fire.

Cheryl gave birth to Marty when she was just nineteen. She was a dancer who sometimes sang backing vocals in a couple of Motown cover bands. Larry was born a year later, Irish twins. Their father was a keyboardist named Greg with Communist leanings and a lustrous mane of copper hair. Perhaps they tried to make it work until it got too hard; he left when Marty was too young to remember. Larry got the hair. Marty's hair was thin and mousy like their mother's, impossible to style.

Sometimes when they visit the nursing home Marty brushes it, running the brush slowly through the wispy strands. It's such a simple act but it feels enormous, their roles reversed: the child acting parent, the parent acting child. That they might have only years or even months before she is unable to recognise them, unable to call Marty by name, is terrifying. There are so many things to say, and not enough time or energy left to say them.

Marty is used to saying their mother reared them casually, their childhood lacked structure, it was fun until it wasn't. But driving into Mallacoota, as the last bend in the road gave onto the outskirts of town, it occurred to them that there were actually times in their childhood they considered happy. The myths they had created were representative, but perhaps they were not the whole truth.

And for whatever reason, the desire to catch a flatty renewed itself with fresh intensity.

THE LODGE IS CROWDED with people counting down. The band stops playing to join in, clapping their hands in time to the passing seconds: *Ten ... nine ... eight*; Hinemoana clutches Marty and shouts along, but Marty's voice won't come, *seven ... six ... five*; Marty is transported, if that's the right word, back to a party at Larry's share house on New Year's Eve, 2004.

Five days earlier the Boxing Day Tsunami killed over two hundred thousand people in Southeast Asia. Marty was still living with their mother in a rental flat in Adelaide, had just turned twenty-one. They watched the devastation on the news with awful fascination, air-con blaring, eating leftovers from Christmas until they felt sick. Cheryl claimed that on the morning it happened, right before it came on the news, she dreamed of a tall wave moving silently between two cliffs. Marty didn't believe her. She was always making stuff up.

At the party, Whitney Houston was playing. Marty's mother was outside smoking joints with some of Larry's friends, and Larry was consoling the girl he liked because she'd just had a fight with her boyfriend. Marty usually hated parties and felt responsible for everyone there, especially their mother and Larry, but tonight seemed different. There were lots of people in the house and Marty walked from room to room feeling wildly anonymous, as if they could be anyone they chose.

Toward midnight they were sniffing amyl on the dance-floor with a bunch of gays when this compact Polynesian chick with brown skin and really long hair danced up to them, singing at the top of her lungs. She grabbed Marty and pulled them into a kind of shuffling, bouncing embrace, singing loudly in their ear. Everyone was wasted, shouting the lyrics more than singing them, but even though this stranger was inhaling noxious gases and swigging tequila from the bottle like everybody else, Marty was struck by Hinemoana's perfect pitch.

'You have a really great voice,' Marty shouted.

'You stole my outfit,' she shouted back.

'What?'

'I *said*, you *stole* my *outfit*,' she yelled. 'Look!'

Hinemoana stepped back and Marty's eyes travelled the length of her until they reached her legs. They weren't that long, but they were shapely. Marty felt their stomach drop.

'How weird is that?! Where the hell did you get yours?'

'I got—' Marty's vision was swimming.

'I stole mine from my sister,' she shouted. 'No, wait. I got them from Savers.'

'You're not going to believe this,' yelled Marty, for the music was still pumping, 'but I found mine on the side of the road.'

'Hallelujah, it's fate!'

Marty was a good foot taller, but although they looked very different on their different bodies, there was no denying the two of them were wearing the *exact same fucking pants*.

'I'm Henny,' she shouted.

'*Ten . . . nine . . . eight*—' the party counted.

'Should we?' she asked.

'*Seven . . . six . . . five*—' Marty was too wasted and impressed to respond. It didn't matter, because the girl wearing Marty's pants pulled them in and kissed them as the clock ticked over and the gays blew party horns, and someone handed round a tray of shots, and suddenly the track changed and everyone cheered because it was Kylie Minogue.

The next morning Marty dropped round to help Larry and his mates clean up.

'Saw you getting cosy with that Hinemoana last night,' said Larry, sweeping bottle caps into a dustpan, a joint hanging from his bottom lip.

'Get fucked, Laz,' said Marty lightly. 'Nah. She's really nice.'

'Got a wicked singing voice. Did you hear her sing? Her entire family is like some famous blues dynasty in New Zealand.'

He emptied the dustpan into a wheelie bin. 'Think you'll see her again?'

'I don't know. Maybe.'

'I can see you two together, weirdly. She'd be good for you. Teach you how to have fun.'

Marty threw an empty bottle at his head. But secretly, they hoped their brother was right.

Now Marty's scalp prickles when they remember how everyone at the party had screamed *four ... three ... two ... one,* and twenty years later Hinemoana kisses them on the lips, swaying a little as the band playing at the lodge goes into a slow one, drawing couples onto the dance floor and forcing all the singles to the sides.

Larry inserts himself between them so they form a circle, arms linked around each other's shoulders. They put their foreheads together and close their eyes. 'I love you guys,' says Larry. 'I think we need to—'

'Alright then, you big softies,' says Hen quickly. 'That's enough.'

'Fucking hell,' says Larry. 'I'm going to find a drink. You want one, Marty?'

'Sure. I'll have a beer.'

'You want one Hen?' he sneers.

Hinemoana widens her eyes and looks from Marty to Larry. The music changes to a funk number, a poor approximation of 'Get Up Offa That Thing.'

'Oi remember this Marty,' goes Laz, suddenly dancing, 'remember Mum used to do it with that guy, what was his name ... Big Mike?' Larry dances away, blending with the crowd. 'Ask Hen why she's not drinking,' he yells over his shoulder as he grabs and twirls a lusty blonde.

Hen takes Marty's hand and leads them outside, where it is quiet. 'Sit down,' she instructs, so Marty sits. Hinemoana begins telling Marty how crushed she was after the last round of IVF. Marty knows they should be listening but Henny's voice sounds far away. Hen moves onto something about Marty's mother, disappointment, intimacy, Larry and surprise. She says words like *accident* and *unexpected*. Marty's not listening, can't concentrate on the sounds.

Instead they scrutinise the sparkly hotpants she is wearing, an unlikely bargain discovered at the op shop yesterday. They feel the scenes colliding in their mind: New Year's Eve, 2004. New Year's Eve, now. *I got them from Savers.* Her voice, her perfect pitch. *The exact same fucking pants.* Inside the lodge, the band has finished their set and a DJ is playing Kylie Minogue. *Can't get you outta my head.* Someone hands round shots. *Like fate or something.* Marty looks down and almost sees them both wearing those pants again. They were made from tent-like material and zipped off at the thighs. The thighs. There is something sensual in the revelation of her thick, powerful thighs.

'Those shorts look great on you, Hen.'

'What the fuck Marty. Did you hear what I just said?'

Maybe Marty heard it. Maybe, they wished they hadn't.

'Marty. This is serious. Be serious, please.'

'It's the third thing,' says Marty.

'What the hell?'

'The third bad thing,' Marty repeats. 'It's the last one for the year.'

The moon is out. It is close to full, and for a second the sprawling grounds of the lodge and the entire lake are lit up silver. Then a cloud engulfs the moon and suddenly it pours with rain.

They think of their mother, how she loved a sudden change of mood. If she were here she would have run into the downpour, stripped off naked and shouted for everyone to come outside. The last time Marty visited the nursing home, Cheryl interrupted their scheduled session of reminiscence therapy, looked at them with sparkling eyes and in a moment of pure lucidity, said, 'Can you believe I still want simply, madly, to *live*?'

Hinemoana tries dragging Marty out of the rain, but Marty shakes her off and stumbles into the downpour.

'Marty!' she yells, but her voice is drowned out.

DOWN AT THE JETTY it is peaceful. The rain has stopped and now the bush releases its perfume. There is a word for this smell, Marty knows it: *petrichor*. They think Larry told them once. He has a lot of random knowledge gleaned from conversations on his Sunday radio show, *Kick Ons With Larry*, which mostly involves him and various guests talking shit while getting stoned. It has the most subscribers of any show on the entire station and is still running after fifteen years. People love listening to him, the way his mind works, the weird places it goes. Larry is basically an idiot, but he has his moments of brilliance.

Thinking of Larry makes their heart race. They are probably in shock. They do and do not understand what Hinemoana has just told them. The rain has raised a mist over the lake and everything seems shrouded in mystery. Suddenly Marty sprints to the jetty, stopping just before they crash into the water. They teeter on the edge for a few seconds, panting, staring at the drop.

'Hey lady,' says a thin, nasally voice behind them. 'Are you alright?'

A tiny man emerges from the mist. Tendrils of sound drift down from the party. There is a boat tied to the jetty with a pelican sitting on top and Marty thinks again of their mother, of the stuffed version of this bird she sleeps with nowadays. They don't know where it came from, it just appeared one day in her hands. It's normal, says the neurologist; many people experiencing cognitive decline find comfort in holding or sleeping with a soft toy. The pelican is kind of cute. For some reason, it's the hardest thing to take.

'How's the serenity?' says the little man, walking toward them on the jetty. 'Not worried you're missing out on the party?'

As he approaches Marty sees he's wearing a flannel shirt. He is shorter than Hinemoana, tanned and mousy. His head is shaved but there's a foot-long rat tail dangling from his nape. He twirls it round his index finger while he speaks and every now and then he brushes the split ends across his lips.

'Me and the boys are just about to have a fish. You should join us.'

'Right now?'

'Yeah, why not? It's New Year's Day baby! Let's go catch the first fish of the year!'

More men appear on the jetty. They look about the same age as Marty, all wearing the same uniform as the tiny man in front. Flannos, runners, shorts and caps with serious-looking sunnies perched atop the brims. One of them carries an Esky. Another has a bundle of rods tucked beneath his arm. One brings the tackle box. The rest carry nets and torches, a stack of buckets and a spotlight.

'Okay,' says Marty, 'I'll come.'

'You beauty,' says the little guy. 'There's the boat,' he points to the one with the pelican. 'Get in.'

Marty waits for the men to load in all their gear. With each body, the boat sits a little flatter on the water. Just as Marty is readying themself to leap from the jetty, the little guy stops them. 'Wait,' he says. 'First thing's first. We need to introduce ourselves.' He says it with great ceremony. 'I'm Nibbles. And this is Brendan, Scotty, Simmo, Mick and Aloysius, would you believe it, his mother named him after a bloody priest. They may look like your typical drunken idiots, but they're serious fisherman, this lot.'

'Who's driving?' asks Marty.

'Who's driving!? I thought you were going to ask why they call me Nibbles.'

'Oh. Okay, why?'

'*Because*,' he says, pausing for effect.

His mates titter.

'*Because ...*'

'Go on Nibbles, tell her,' say his mates.

Nibbles looks Marty directly in the eye and says, 'Because I'm so good at nibbling on the pussy!'

The men piss themselves laughing. Marty stares. They have to hand it to the guy for novelty – they've never heard that one before.

'Right. So ... are we going out to catch a fish?'

'Too bloody right we are,' says Nibbles as the engine splutters and the smell of petrol floods the air. Marty laughs because there's nothing else for it. And why did Nibbles use the definite article: so good at nibbling on *the* pussy, instead of just nibbling pussy? And what the fuck is nibbling, anyway?

'Call it Nibbles's famous intuition,' he yells over the engine noise, 'but I have a good feeling we'll catch a few flatties tonight!'

BOAT SOUNDS: LAPPING, SLOSHING, the roar of the motor and the windy vacuum at speed, the whine of fishing lines strung taut and made to slice and sing in the wind. The lake is tenebrous and silky, and as Nibbles propels them through the darkness Marty feels their mind slowly empty of thoughts. For the first time in months, they feel almost peaceful.

Nibbles cuts the engine and suddenly all is quiet. They do not anchor but drift instead across the sands, a better way to catch a flathead. Rods are passed around and they bait up. Nobody speaks as one by one they cast their lines into the water, watching them sink beneath the caliginous lake.

The night waxes. They listen. One of Nibbles's mates opens the Esky he's been sitting on and hands out cans of beer. Everything is soft and blurred, but the calm is edged by a tense excitement running through their fingertips, electrifying their lines and sparking where it hits the water. There's a twinge on Marty's: three quick, successive jabs. They wait. Then there is the shock of the fish taking bait; Marty leans back, reeling, astonished by the fish's desire to escape.

Their fight is tense and thrilling. The fish struggles, gives up, finds the strength to go again. They brace themself against the boat as line screams through the reel. There is a sharp, still quiet; the men do not cheer or swear but give Marty space, respectful of a battle they believe is almost sacred. Some of them are busy with their own fish. The floor is slick with brine and blood and whatever sand and weed the flatties dredged up from the deep. All adrenaline, finally, they haul their catch into the boat.

The flathead gasps on the deck. It is a slick, dark monster. Instead of fawn and sandy brown it is a deep, black-green. Like a rhino, its skin is thick and scarred. Everyone stares as it struggles. The dark around them is complete and for a second Marty feels a sharp, intense moment of kinship with the men, the water and this incredible, pulsing fish.

'Look at that,' says Nibbles. 'That's gotta be the biggest flatty I've ever seen.'

'I can't believe it.'

'Believe it! When they're big like this it means they're breeders.'

'I can't believe ...' but Marty is talking about something else, for it is only now that they allow themself to fully comprehend what Henny told them at the lodge. It is unbelievable, or perhaps another one of Larry's brilliant moments: as crazy as it sounds, Marty can almost picture Henny, Larry and the baby – *the* baby, definite article – who will have Henny's legs and Larry's mind and their mother's infallible zest for living ...

Where does that leave Marty?

'Yep ...' says Nibbles, surveying the fish in wonder, 'she's a big old girl. Hey pretty lady,' he says tenderly, 'I reckon you've got a few more generations in you yet. Here we go. Let's throw her back.'

But Marty has already grasped the struggling fish and yanked the big hook from her gullet, has heard the splash and marvelled at how fast she slipped away.

A LOOK OF
EXTREME FESTIVITY

WHEN YOU TURNED EIGHTEEN, around the same time you finished your exams, you and Jules got in the river. It was only September and still too cold for swimming, but it didn't matter that the water would be freezing, high and swollen with the snowmelt. You stripped off quickly, squealing as you waded through the swathes of wattle which lay thick and pale on the surface, trembling like the foam afloat a pint of lager. The smell was powerful and brought on Jules's hay fever. He sneezed, stumbled and plunged beneath the water.

The current was strong; you couldn't tell where he had gone. The sudden panic took your breath away. You swung around but only saw the river, so green that day, the white and yellow flowers and your skin bright in the glare. A kingfisher flashed blue. The sun was sharp and rarefied. What would it be like to lose him? There was no time to wonder, for suddenly a cry bounced off the steep red bank and Jules resurfaced, laughing, wiping wattle from his eyes.

How similar you had been that spring, lean and pale, your limbs jangly and your muscles tense, two fledglings on the precipice of flight. You were leaving childhood, angling toward the future. You had matching freckles and plans to leave town. The river left a pleasant chill upon your skin and as you slowly picked your way back up the hill you felt connected to your brother in a strong, simple way; a moment of kinship you'd have trouble holding onto.

It is a complicated thing, having your own mirror wandering through the world. Even fraternal twins must constantly negotiate their separation. You and Jules were look-alikes, uncanny doubles, yet as much as you resembled one another, the doubling only amplified your differences. You were sensitive and conscientious, always seeking approbation. All your life, people have relied on you to do things well. Jules was impetuous and stubborn, mysterious in a way that felt like a refusal. As much as you tried, you never really got to know him.

At the end of school you topped your year. The principal was shocked that someone with no sciences had gotten dux. Jules did badly. He hadn't even bothered with half of his exams. In his mind he had already started wandering; he had gotten what your mother called an urge for going, quoting a Joni Mitchell song. You had never liked this song because its yearning made you feel like there was something you were missing, some deep desire or longing that you simply didn't have. Everyone else had it – your mother, your father, Jules. They wanted life to mirror their romantic aspirations, but you just wanted to get out of the valley and study something sensible, like law.

Jules followed you to Melbourne, where he hung around your college dorm and tried to pick up some of your new friends. When they made it clear they were not interested, he disappeared. You didn't hear from him for months, until he turned up at a party telling stories of a woman with a campervan. His hair was dirty and his face looked oddly tanned.

For the next fifteen years or so he wandered in and out of your life, arriving at random before leaving again. It wasn't the separation which pained you so much as grappling with this constant state of flux; just as soon as you got used to him he'd disappear, leaving you to sort things out.

Like the girlfriend who once screamed at you, just fucking tell me if he's dumped me. Like the guys who rocked up at your house, demanding money. Like the detectives who once questioned you about a load of small blue pills imprinted with the word DOG, the G appearing backward, so no one knew if it was supposed to say DOG or GOD, Jules's idea of a joke. You said you'd never heard of them; didn't even know where he was. Good pills though – you took too many at a party once and spent the entire evening lying on the loungeroom floor, pressing buttons on a remote, trying to get in touch with him, thinking it was your phone.

Meanwhile, all his fines arrived at your address.

You saved them up and waited for such time that he would reappear. At the end of undergrad you applied for a masters, not in law but in botany, studying the perfect forms of cells and seeds you had discovered in the archives accidentally, between boring lectures about torts. You finished uni, got a job in research, worked a bit, met a man, had two babies, went back to work and tried not to think about Jules. Your father died and you stopped talking to your mother, and still you didn't hear from him. He sent a postcard from India once: he was living in Hyderabad; he didn't say why.

But you kept remembering that day with the wattle, when you recognised him in some profound, important way. Hard to decide what it meant, though it wasn't really urgent. You would think about it later, and know what to feel then.

And one day he came back.

Another brilliant morning, this time in July, the seasons having shifted slightly so that by midwinter all the wattles in your suburb had burst forth in yellow sprays. For a long time afterward, it was one of those things you kept returning to, unable to put down. It formed an uneasy pair to the river memory, how the knock cracked sharply in the weekday quiet and then there was Jules, standing in the doorway looking thin, thinner and lighter and somehow more brilliant than you'd ever seen him.

'Who told you where I lived?' you asked.

'Do you ever think about Christmas? Those cicada shells we painted gold and silver.'

You both performed your alchemy on other things – gumnuts, pine cones, rocks – but none looked so mysterious as those gilded shells, which clung to the boughs of the Christmas tree with a spooky look of sentience.

'They freaked me out, you know. How certain lights would animate them and they'd start to creep around.'

'Is that why you're here – to talk about Christmas?'

'Doesn't matter,' he said. 'Are you going to let me come in?'

You stood between him and the entrance, knowing that admitting him would only amount to watching him go again. 'Why should I?'

And behind him now the tree blazed green and yellow, the calls of wattlebirds like little motors spluttering in the branches. The heady smell. How the riot of the blossoms looked extremely festive, which was out of keeping with his news.

The cancer started in his lungs and now it was in his bones.

'Which ones?' you asked.

'All of them.' He touched a finger lightly to his sternum.

You winced. 'What'll you do?'

'Die, I guess.' He laughed breathlessly, the sound like wind in eucalyptus leaves. 'What else is there? I'm going to try and stay out of hospital. I've decided I want to be at home.'

Where is home, you wanted to ask, and how have you been living? And who do you love and why and what made you come back from wherever it is you've been?

But speech stuck in your throat; you found yourself staring past him at the wattle tree.

'I'm living up at Dad's,' he continued. 'I kept thinking you'd show up, like, wanting to check on the house.'

'I don't like going there,' you said. 'It's not exactly luxury accommodation.'

'I guess not,' said Jules. Pushing the gate, he stepped onto the street. A wind had gotten up and yellow flowers skittered on the footpath, turning to dust at his feet. As you watched him walk away, you thought of all the other times you'd stood in this position. Just as Jules was prone to going, you were never good at leaving – never knew how or when to leave, or where the fuck to go. At the first sign of his departure you would dig your heels in, stubborn as a goat.

But now you found yourself pushing the gate, calling after him, 'Jules, wait. I'm coming with you.'

At least you could give him your witness, which you meant to do until the end.

THEN THERE WERE THE dying weeks, Jules propped up against the pillows in the bed they wheeled into his loungeroom, delirious on morphine. Once he sat straight up and said, 'I should have done it. I should have just *gone* there. I regret it, you know? I never liked that fucker, Dougall. He tried to tell me it was sugar. When her adult ones came down, they grew over the top of her baby teeth. Right over the top, just like a little shark.'

You watched him try to stick a small round bandaid, which he believed to be radioactive, onto a cup, a banana, his oxygen tank and finally, his shoe.

He said he wasn't going to tell ASIO what you'd done. 'I'm good at keeping secrets,' he said, tapping the side of his nose like in a film of old. 'I've been keeping them all my life.'

He saw the nurses as cartoon bears with big syringes, dancing happily. 'I'm on the F-Train,' he cried ecstatically, referring to the fentanyl now scudding through his veins.

'I loved her you know,' he said another time. 'But I never told her, stupid me.'

Sometimes in his delirium or sleep, he'd say a woman's name. 'Priya,' he would moan. 'Priya … please.'

You wanted to record the things he said like clues in a detective show, so that later you could read back over them and piece together his existence. But you never got a pen and paper, and you wondered if this was because you didn't really want to know.

On the phone one night, you told Leo that you had prepared yourself for news of Jules's death finding its way to you from somewhere distant, across land or oceans, from the other side of the world. In your imagination it was always something hard and fast – an accident or suicide, an overdose or sudden illness. But his cancer was just painful and mundane. There were days you couldn't look at him, worried he would see your face and know that you were disappointed.

When you were kids your mother spent longer than seemed usual on a PhD in modernist poetry. *The imperfect is our paradise,* she would say, reading Wallace Stevens, *note that, in this bitterness, delight.* It suited her to think that people were essentially chaotic, that living was desiring and desiring was restlessness and lack. When she left your father for a doctor in town, married him and built a home and painted it all white, you felt disappointed in your mother in a way you'd not expected. You were angry with her for leaving you to raise your sad, dysfunctional dad alone, but more than that, you were angry that she'd not done something more spectacular.

'Everyone gets cancer,' Jules said during a rare moment of clarity, his eyes fixed on your face. 'I'm not afraid of dying. I'm afraid of all the things I'm missing. I'm worried I haven't lived a good life, haven't lived right by people, haven't lived right by myself. I'm scared it will hurt. When it comes, I want you to pump me full of drugs. Overdose me, I'm serious. I don't want to fucking know.'

Then he closed his eyes and rested.

During this time, you dreamed of animals. Black dogs and other beasts that stalked behind you on the back roads. Horses whinnying and bucking in the wind, synchronised and weirdly fluid, changing ways like schools of silver fish. A panther with its den of bones. A nanny goat with two grey kids in tow, offering them her teats. In the dream you felt the predator around you as they suckled, the need to feed your babies sparring with the need to stay alive. At the end of the dream there was a sound like stone or metal; the sound would startle you awake.

You would look around the room that you and Jules had shared as children, at the cobwebs and the ancient Blu Tack on the walls. In the corner, an antique ebony wardrobe still bore stickers handed out at school and ones you'd found in show bags, the fairies and the stars and Daffy Duck and *Magic Happens* and the one you'd gotten from the CFA where koalas dressed as firefighters told you to *crawl low in smoke*. There were others, ones that Mrs Myrtle stuck to your piano sheets which said *Eyes on the Music*, you were lazy, you always tried to play by ear. Jules was better. He actually bothered learning how to read. The riot of memories made you feel crazy – too many stimuli. Sleep punctured by Jules crying in the night. And then the raucous calls of gang-gangs in the hazelnut tree, just as soon as dawn arrived.

There were other things, too. Daily drop-ins from palliative care, learning how to help the nurses turn him over, protect his heels and hips from bedsores, flush his IV lines, give him morphine, help him shit. At first these tasks repelled you, the intimacy with your brother's body, the awful smells. But you adapted, performing your tasks with determination and, at times, amazement. It was both exalted and banal to care for him as he was dying – ordinary and yet full of grace.

HIS WIFE MADE DINNER and made sure that you were sleeping, but she kept her distance from his body, patting his hand and then retreating as though she was afraid to break him. You settled into your separate roles, her keeping house and you keeping vigil. You hadn't even known that he was married, but this was something you became accustomed to along with everything else. His wife was from the Mitta Valley, some girl who had sold him a nanny goat to keep the blackberries down.

'Me and her moved in at pretty much the same time,' she laughed. 'Fucken funny, aye. I don't know which of us he liked better. He loved that fucken goat. I'm more of a Horse Girl, y'know?'

'Where is she now? The goat.'

'Escaped,' said Horse Girl. 'Chewed through her rope and fucked off up the hill somewhere.'

You felt the dream around you like a premonition, though you weren't sure what part of the future it foretold. 'I suppose she's somewhere in the high country,' you mused.

'Yeah, you see them up there now. I saw a massive female keeping up with a herd of brumbies once, acting like a horse and that. She had this big shaggy white coat and ran like the fucken wind. The dogs tend to keep them down. But then your farmers have the right to shoot the dogs, and once the dogs are down the goats get back up. They breed like fucken rabbits. I should know.'

'You breed goats?'

'Tried it once. Never again.'

She showed you pictures of the wedding at her parents' stables: Jules looking weirdly benign in this camp cowboy get-up and Horse Girl trailing a veil over the homely arse of a big bay mare.

'When was this?' you asked.

'A while ago now,' she said. 'Two and a half, three years.'

His wife was a practical woman with the generous thighs of equestrian types everywhere. When you had nothing more to say to one another, she fled out to the paddocks with her mares. You watched them chasing clouds of gnats across the long, wet grasses and your grief turned to impatience, and you began to wish your brother would just hurry up and die.

Then when death finally came it was a long, wet gasp, and you and his wife sat across from each other listening to the shudder and the stop.

Afterward, you missed him. It was unexpected, a physical shock. There had been no reconciliation, no final words. The last thing he said to you was, 'Fuck ... this.' You said nothing. In the presence of his pain, how hard Jules had to work to die, the things you'd planned on saying had seemed overly contrived.

Horse Girl had a strong, clear manner of expressing her emotions. 'Well this fucken hurts,' she said earnestly, her cheeks wet with tears. 'I wasn't prepared for it to hurt this much.' She cried and cooked and raged and rode her horses, making calls and doing all the practical things that needed to be done. You walked around the house in a stupor, shuffling Jules's unfinished compositions, fingering his knick-knacks and forgetting to drink the cups of tea she made.

Sometimes you looked at her and felt resentful of her easy access to her grief. She wanted to know how you were feeling. How could you explain that all your life you'd hated it when people treated you and Jules as though you were a single entity, when the most rudimentary assessment should reveal the opposite was true. But you realised now that you'd relied on Jules for contrast. From here on, anything you needed to know about yourself would have to be gleaned without him. You were a single entity. Things would never be the same.

'What are you going to do now?' asked Horse Girl, the night before the funeral.

'I don't know. Go back to Melbourne, I guess. What about you?'

'No point staying here. I mean, the house belongs to you. I'll probably go back and live with my parents for a bit. It'll be good for me, there's lots to do. I'll keep busy with the horses.'

'I'm sorry. I don't want you to feel you have to move. Take as much time as you want. You could stay here for a while?'

Horse Girl looked at you kindly. 'That's alright,' she said. 'Jules wouldn't want me to wallow. He was always moving. He'd want me to do the same.'

On the morning of the funeral it was raining and the mountains shied away behind long shrouds of heavy vapour. The pump, which had been sketchy lately finally clapped out, so there would be no cleansing shower and no water for your tea. You and Horse Girl dressed as best you could, doused yourselves in perfume and then drove together to the hall in town, where you gave your elegies with smudgy eyes, smelling strongly of *Fantasy* by Britney Spears – her choice – your hair full of sleep and horses, and a wild sort of relief.

You saw her one more time to scatter Jules's ashes. Unexpected: how they skittered over the green river, borne by a sudden wind. And the wattle she threw in after, how Jules would have hated it, it would have made him sneeze. It turned circles on the current, bright and buoyant, and you wanted to laugh loudly at the absurdity of the thing.

How festive, you thought.

A wave of affection for Horse Girl overcame you.

ON CHRISTMAS EVE, THREE months after Jules's death, you find yourself at the house again, thinking of the goat. It gives you a menacing feeling to imagine her in the high plains, evading wild dogs which are themselves evading farmers, shots ringing out and echoing off rocks. The land belongs to none of them. And you – what are you doing in this house of loss?

Your half-acre block sits in the long furrow between mountains. This is Jaitmatang Country, in the foothills of Mount Bogong. The mountain peaks are brown in summer, sloping purple in the afternoon. There is a quick green river; paddocks backed by knots of dense, blue bush. There are many remarkable things about the landscape – all angles, shadow, sky – but it's the trees that move you, the stands of silver snow gum, alpine ash and peppermint; black sallee, baby bluegum, and every type of wattle tree. There is alpine wattle with its pale blooms and honey scent. Ovens wattle with the sharp, serrated leaves that look like mossy teeth. Golden wattle shedding dust that flows in rivers when it's wet, a tide which floods the porch your parents paved themselves and laps at the back door.

Christmas Eve is rainy. You stand at the back door and then cross over to the other side, where Leo is supervising as the girls tie carrots to the verandah. The dogs wait patiently, thinking that the carrots are for them. Marta, who is five, seems to have a comprehensive plan. She is a classic older child: clever, sensitive, impatient with the things she cannot understand. In some ways, she is easier to get along with. But Evie, the younger one, can sometimes be mysterious. She holds herself at a distance from you, Leo and her sister in a way that makes you think of Jules.

Just before he died you brought them here to see him. It was the first time Jules had met your children. Marta kissed him shyly and then sat by the bed, dutifully reading him her books. But Evie marched right up and slapped her hand down on his forehead. 'He's boiling,' she cried. 'Feel his head!' She stroked him for a moment, ear tilted to his face. Then she came over and planted herself in your lap.

'He said he's sorry.'

Jules lay there unconscious, his face blazing with sepsis from the final bout of pneumonia he simply couldn't shake.

'When did he say that?' you asked your daughter.

'Just then.'

'But he's sleeping, Bub. I was right here. I didn't hear him.'

She stroked your hair. 'Mummy,' she said. 'He told me in my mind.'

You couldn't fathom it. And there were other spooky goings-on, a tinkle of bells in the middle of the night. The sense that someone was standing on the doormat waiting, although they wouldn't come inside. You didn't think you were a superstitious person, but since being here for Christmas you've kept all the doors and windows open so that anyone who might be passing through can keep on moving to the other side.

Now you hear Marta saying, 'I'm certain the reindeer will like these carrots. Don't you think so, Evie?'

She has just learned the word certain and is applying it to everything. She's certain it will rain today. She's certain her swimming has got better since her lessons. She's certain she is five and Evie's three.

'Maybe,' says Leo. 'Let's hope they know where to find us.'

'No, I'm certain. As certain as can be.'

'Certain, Daddy,' mimics Evie, tying a carrot next to one of Marta's.

'Not like that Evie,' she says, guiding her sister to another post. 'Put it here.'

You watch them with a sweet, strange amusement. They are still your babies, not yet self-conscious, young enough to be attached to you. In some ways you don't see them; they are so much still a part of you that it's like looking at yourself. But the more you watch them, the less you know. At times like these they can be strangely separate and officious; you know that one day they will grow apart and leave you, and you will feel a mix of longing and relief.

You walk past them, out into the rain. The drops are falling softly now, falling on the leaves and stems of plants and flowers growing wildly in the garden. After the goat left, Jules stopped bothering to keep the grass or blackberries down. He let black wattle crop up everywhere, saplings crowding out the apple trees. Once Christmas is over and done with, whether or not you decide to stay, you will have to come here with a backhoe and start mowing it all down.

But now the rain makes silver floss atop the wattle's feathered, fern-like leaves, which shake on you as you pass under. They have exchanged their blossoms for the bumpy, distended pods of seeds. Before you go inside you pick one up on impulse. Then you carry it into your bedroom, placing it beneath your pillow for the night.

That afternoon, Leo takes the kids into town to catch the shops before they close. You go into the bedroom, open the wardrobe and slip into one of Jules's jackets, the mangy linen one he wore as a kind of dressing gown. It smells of his body, of Nag Champa incense and a smell you've come to recognise as cancer, and the thought of your own clothes hanging next to it is abject and unbearable. His clothing, you think, is the hardest to get rid of. You put the jacket back on its hanger and close the wardrobe door.

In the shed you find mysterious articles in a wooden box. You open it slowly, holding your breath. Inside there is a photograph of an Indian woman smoking a joint with a quirky smile, her arms heavy with a huge ginger cat. There is an orange pierced with fragrant cloves, an obscure book of poetry with faded marginalia, a little gauze bag containing two baby teeth. Who is that woman? Whose are those teeth? It is disturbing to think your twin's secret life is shouting at you through these objects, though you have no way now of deciphering their import.

You try to remember any of the things Jules said when he was high, but there are too many spaces to fill in, too many gaps, and eventually you put the articles back inside their box.

'What have you been up to?' asks Leo when he comes home, smiling, as though you have been doing something shifty.

'Nothing,' you say. 'I went for a walk.'

Later, the girls re-check their carrots and then put beer and shortbread out for Santa. These rituals, which up 'til now you've never really looked at, seem both inevitable and out of place here in your childhood home. Once the girls are in bed, you and Leo get a bit drunk laying out the presents. You have some silly festive sex, which is fun until afterward, when he holds you tightly like you're something precious he's decided to protect.

As you lie there in his arms, desire folds up and packs off somewhere chilly. At the beginning, just after Jules had died, you wanted to have sex with Leo all the time. You felt greedy, hungrier than you had ever felt. You wanted brightly coloured vegetables and bloody meat. You wanted giving and receiving. It had something, you thought, to do with life. Affirming it. Loving it. Wanting to feel and eat and fuck it in the face of death.

'But aren't you sad?' asked Leo.

'Of course I'm sad. I'm constantly in pain.'

'So? I don't get it.'

You tried to explain. So Leo stroked your face and took you back to bed, but the way he touched you felt wrong, like he was afraid you'd break apart beneath his hands.

Gently, you pushed him off. 'Never mind,' you would say, lying there and feeling starving.

Since then, the sex has been infrequent. But for a second tonight it seemed that things were back on track.

'I love you,' says Leo softly.

'We should probably go to sleep.'

As you wait for sleep you look around the room inside your mind and feel as though you're back within the dying weeks or maybe even back here as a child. Probate has come through and now the house is yours, but it's a difficult inheritance, with lots to do to make it liveable. You're not sure whether you will sell it and move on or, as Leo not-so-secretly desires, whether you will move up here yourself.

It's not a bad idea; your girls may benefit from growing up in the country. But still, the thought of it repels you. The valley is a crazy place, backward, full of grief. There is only one road in and out. People come here to avoid things. The town is full of racists. There are secrets, gossip; something said in confidence becomes public property overnight. There is the spike of cortisol every time you have to go into the supermarket. People will recognise you – there will be things they want to know.

Leo tries his best to convince you that it's going to be different. He wonders if the town has changed, become more modern. He claims to have seen some cool people out the front of the café. It will be a new chapter, he says, without the stress of city life, somewhere to process everything that's happened. He emphasises *process*, which makes you think you have been doing it all wrong.

You know where he is coming from. Leo grew up in the city and is romanced by everything he sees, drinking in the country with his city eyes and feeling nostalgic for a thing he never had. His sentimentality makes you wary. You watched your parents sink beneath their pastoral dream, the reality of such places being inconsistent with their idle contemplation. You do not want to do what they did. You do not want to end up like them.

Even before they separated, there was always something going wrong. Your parents resented all the things they couldn't finish on the house, the threat of termites and the fact that bushfires put a premium on insurance. They resented the notion that the land on which they'd settled just refused to go their way. Blackberries everywhere. Black wattle everywhere. Wombats digging under fences, possums in the roof. Rats in the walls, weevils in the flour, brown snakes in the house, millipedes in autumn, blow-flies in summer, starlings in the eaves, European wasps, gum leaves in the gutters, silt in the pipes, possum shit and cow shit in the water that you drank and washed in. The place refused to be managed, and yet your parents refused to admit how tenuous their hold on it really was.

You tell Leo that one summer, when the house began to smell of rotting meat, your dad found a pattern in the dirt and followed it to where a kangaroo had dragged itself beneath the house to die, the flesh now liquefied and mag-got blown, ants swarming in the crater of its eye.

There has been so much death and failure here. You need him to understand that you've been left with a com-promised and compromising legacy; you don't know how to hold it, or what to do. You want for there to be an answer, for there to be an end to your confusion and unease.

During the night you dream of childhood, of Jules and swimming and the calls of wild dogs. Of swirling parties, your mother and your father entertaining people at the house. Of stealing the Christmas tree from a rich, stingy neighbour; driving up the dirt track in your father's Peu-geot 505, the handsaw lying in your mother's lap. You smell the cut and then the sap comes out like semen, and from the semen monstrous insects grow. They shake their gold and sil-ver wings and dance and glitter madly, glancing off the walls in pricks of light. You open doors which lead to other scenes. They seem to go on endlessly; these strange, haunted dreams.

You wake up sweating, the sheet tangled round your legs. Both your daughters have somehow wormed their way between you and you teeter on the very edge of the bed. Marta flings her hand across your chest, laughing in her sleep.

'Is that Marta?' asks Leo groggily. 'What's she dreaming about?

'I don't know.'

You can feel him smiling. 'Such a little freak.'

As you try again to sleep, you think that maybe it's okay not knowing. It's okay to leave the house unfinished, your mourning unfinished, to do it wrongly, to do it weird. It is no good looking for conclusions. You thought that Jules's death would settle something – you would recognise him finally, and in knowing him you'd also know yourself. But maybe it's okay to let it go. You will work things out eventually; it doesn't have to happen now.

As you drift back into sleep, you think you hear a bleat. You cannot know that outside, beneath the big bright sky, something is occurring. It comes to you from down the lane, on hoof and mane, pelts shiny in the moonglow. They look like something else entirely, less animal than omen. They will stamp and whinny and then a few among them will begin to eat. Leaping the fence, they plough into your garden. You stir, go back to sleep. When that is stripped they creep up like demented reindeer for the carrots that your girls have tied to the verandah; the sound of their hooves is what wakes you, sometime around five.

CHRISTMAS DAY IS BLUSH behind the mountains. In the valley, the air is dim and still. Hearing a noise, you get out of bed and open the sliding door. Leo is behind you, flicking on the light. Just there, a foot from where you're standing, the herd materialises from the gloom. A couple of them whinny. Another bleats politely, as if excusing all the noise.

The dogs race out excitedly, yapping at the scent of livestock. They try a bit of herding but they're city mutts and no good for the work. The brumbies scatter, streaming through the apple trees, trampling wattle saplings as they flee. But the nanny goat and her two kids are unperturbed, calmly grazing on their carrots even as the dogs run circles, barking madly, and Leo leaps from the verandah and begins to rush around, undecided whether to shoo them off or bring them in. You watch it all as currents of hilarity rush through your extremities, fizzing in your fingertips and nipples, turning to static in your hair. Leo asks if it is normal for a herd like this to come keen as cousins for Christmas Day's libations and you shake your head, surprised, for you have never seen anything like it.

How have you been living? you could ask. And what does it all mean?

But there will be time for questions later; for now the girls are up and want to know if Santa has been and whether Donna Dancer Prancer Rudolf Blitzen et al have eaten all those carrots they tied to the verandah. They fall silent and survey the herd with eyes like saucers, the brumbies with their rippling flanks and tangled manes. But it's the goat that draws them, standing tall and proud and ugly in the midst of all her elegant, muscular companions. Her shaggy coat is huge and matted, stained a whitish yellow. Evie says it looks like Santa's beard. 'A Christmas goat,' says Marta wisely.

'Certainly,' says Evie.

'Hey, that's my word.'

As if she has heard them, the goat makes an officious bleat and leaps from the verandah, sure of the claim she has made on the day.

'This is madness,' says Leo, panting with exertion. 'What are we going to do?'

You turn to answer him—

But now the girls are getting impatient, so you go inside for presents just as morning spills into the valley, leaving goats and brumbies to deracinate the wild vegetation. A quick wind scatters seedpods and the smell of grazing beasts; it is all extremely festive, and it occurs to you that there is someone who will know exactly how to handle all these interlopers; a practical woman from the next valley whose wedding gown once trailed over the arse end of a bay mare.

And maybe you'll resolve to call her, if you can find her number.

NOTES

ONE OF MY CREATIVE writing teachers said originality is
a redundant category; all contemporary texts are haunted by
each other and this book is no exception.

The epigraphs are from Wallace Stevens's 1942 poem
'Notes Toward a Supreme Fiction,' and Djuna Barnes's 1936
novel *Nightwood*, respectively.

Throughout 'Glimmer' I have drawn phrases, images
and instances from Lorrie Moore's 1985 short story, 'How
to Be an Other Woman,' including when the narrator says
she is 'part of a great hysterical you mean historical tradition.' Other ideas and phrases I have pulled from elsewhere:
'I just liked getting drunk and being in love' is from Eileen
Myles's 1994 novel *Chelsea Girls;* 'the pulsing of a pussy in
great need of fucking' appears in Maggie Nelson's 2009
Bluets; Regina Barecca wrote the line 'humour has a history of belonging to men' in an introduction to the journal
Women's Studies, Volume 15, Issue 4, 1988.

'New Directions' draws on Andy Jackson's essay 'Free Verse Bodies. Or, Is Poetry Deformed?' which appeared online at *Meanjin* on 12 November 2014; some of the lines voiced by the eel are appropriations of Jackson's critical thought on language, bodies and bodies of text. Many of Sigi's lines are directly quoted from Sigmund Freud's letters to his friend Eduard Silberstein, dated between March and May of 1876, translated by Arnold J. Pomerans and collected in Walter Boehlich's 1992 book, *The Letters of Sigmund Freud to Eduard Silberstein 1871-1881*, such as: 'Trieste is a very beautiful city, it's beasts are very beautiful beasts'; 'I shan't write separately to you on how I eat, drink, spend my days. I'd rather report on what I've seen of la bella Italia and how I go with the beast killing science'; 'The sea, which may be seen at all times from my window, is usually as smooth as glass'; ' … the beast killing science, which disturbs me even in my dreams, in my thoughts nothing but the great problems connected with the words ducts, testicles and ovaries, universal words …'. The final sentiment is an appropriation of a similar line in Deborah Levy's 2018 book, *The Cost of Living,* in which she writes, 'It was a big release from the terror of death to finally acknowledge that it is also always absurd.' The line 'every patient yields to the compulsion to repeat, and in such cases where the resistance is greater, the repetition is also greater' is a loose adaptation of similar wording in Freud's 1914 paper 'Remembering, Repeating and Working-Through.'

'Peduncle Slap' takes cues from Hélène Cixous's seminal text, 'The Laugh of the Medusa,' translated by Keith and Paula Cohen in 1976, as well as Adrienne Rich's 1976 book *Of Woman Born;* their thoughts and ideas on women's experience are echoed by the narrator. The line 'the wind performed its frigid ministry,' is a version of a line from Samuel Taylor Coleridge's 1798 poem 'Frost at Midnight,' which reads, 'The Frost performs its secret ministry, / Unhelped by any wind.'

'A Woman, a Man and Another' is a loose adaptation of Freud's famous case study of the witty butcher's wife, as Lacan would later call her. I've drawn on the original 1899 text in the *Interpretation of Dreams* as well as Colette Soler's lecture, 'History and Hysteria: The Witty Butcher's Wife,' published in *NFF* Volume 6, Numbers 1 & 2, 1992.

When Jane cites D.W. Winnicott's essay on psychotic parents in 'The Martini Effect,' she is talking about 'The Effect of Psychotic Parents on the Emotional Development of the Child,' published in *British Journal of Psychiatric Social Work*, Vol. 6, No. 1, 1961.

'Brink Man' contains echoes of Doris Lessing's brilliant story 'One off the Short List' from 1963.

Finally, the line of poetry quoted by the narrator's mother in 'A Look of Extreme Festivity' is from Wallace Stevens's 1942 'The Poems of Our Climate': *'The imperfect is our paradise. / Note that, in this bitterness, delight.'*

ACKNOWLEDGEMENTS

FROM A SKETCHY PROPOSITION to the book it is now, my chiefest thanks are due to my friend, editor and publisher Emily Riches, whose thoughtful consideration, humour and careful shepherding brought it all together. Em, thank you for your diligence, honesty, care, and for your faith in me.

Thanks to The Readings Foundation and The Wheeler Centre, where I was a Hot Desk Fellow in 2022 and where this manuscript really began to take shape. I am grateful to the Mornington Peninsula Shire AiR program for the opportunity to spend two weeks in a rather haunted cottage by the sea. To my teachers and classmates in the Master of Creative Writing, Editing and Publishing, thanks for feedback on the earliest versions of these stories. Thanks are also due to Leo, for his fancy dinners and sage legal advice.

An earlier version of 'New Directions' was runner-up in the 2022 Neilma Sidney Short Story Prize and first appeared in *Overland* online under the title 'New

Directions in Anthropomorphism.' Likewise, an earlier version of 'A Look of Extreme Festivity' was runner up and first appeared on the Olga Masters Short Story Award website in 2022. My gratitude to those publications and to the judges of those prizes.

In 2021 and 2023 my dad and stepdad died of cancer, and although the book is not for them it is definitely of them, and so to Dad and Phil and to their deaths I say, thank you for showing me that mourning doesn't have to be a wasteland; it can be rich and fertile, it can be funny and fecund.

To a bunch of clever, caring people: Chloe, Ella, Ami, Jim, Paddy, Joey, Caito, Sarah, Clare, Charlotte, Mariah, Ben, Chris, Ellen, Francesca, Pucci and Niko; thank you for sharing your stories with me, some of which have inevitably wound up in these pages. It's nice to be held by your humour, energy and intelligence. To my extended family for a sick sense of humour – I hope that all you Reids read this and laugh.

Lastly to Mum, Phoebe and Stella. There is so much to say, but for the moment thank you for your passion, generosity, encouragement, love and inspiration, always. It's been a big few years. I wrote this for us.

MIRIAM WEBSTER's fiction and essays have been published in *Aniko Magazine, HEAT, Island, Overland, The Suburban Review, swim meet lit mag* and certain zines. She is a Wheeler Centre Hot Desk Fellow and her work has been recognised in major prizes including the Calibre Essay Prize, the Neilma Sidney Short Story Prize, the Olga Masters Short Story Award and the inaugural KYD Creative Non-Fiction Essay Prize. She lives in Naarm/Melbourne. *The Slip* is her first book.